Captain Charming

Copyright

Disclaimer

The books in this series are based completely on dreams that I've had or that one of the other people in my relationship has had. They all have a little bit of real life thrown in so that you, the reader, can get to know us a little bit better.

These books can and should be read as standalone books. There isn't an order to them. All of the characters in the books are the same, as they are all based on characters from real life.

As you read these books, please keep in mind that other than the characters and the city they are based in, these books are not connected to other books in the series. They aren't a continuation of other books. They are all novellas based on dreams that revolve around the same characters.

As you keep that in mind, please enjoy reading this book. I do hope you will also read the others in this series and love them as much as I loved writing them!

Opening Quote

Seconds, hours, so many days. You know what you want, but how long can you wait? Every moment lasts forever when you feel you've lost your way. And what if my chances were already gone? I started believing that I could be wrong. But you gave me one good reason to fight and never walk away. So here I am still holding on. With every step you climb another mountain. With every breath it's harder to believe. You make it through the pain, weather the hurricanes, to get to that one thing. Just when you think the road is going nowhere, just when you almost gave up on your dreams, they take you by the hand, and show you that you can. There are no boundaries.

No Boundaries by Adam Lambert

Chapter One

☆ Mariah ☆

Breathe... Just breathe... Three... Deep breath... Let it out... Two...
Deep breath... Let it out... One... Deep breath... Let it out...

I slowly open my eyes. The grip on my steering wheel loosens, but only slightly. I nod to myself as I keep talking myself down, quietly singing along to the radio as I stare at the venue in front of me.

The Depot in Gainesville is such a pretty location for any kind of event. It seems to match the tone of this book signing perfectly. The atmosphere is perfect. It's rustic. I like rustic.

I focus on the calming quiet the Depot exudes. I like quiet. I like calm. I like order. I like everything about this place.

I take another deep breath and cough. I really need to figure out different ways to get my anxiety in check. Sometimes, taking so many deep breaths fucks with my lungs. Too much air. Then my body retaliates viciously and sends me into a coughing fit. Which, of course, causes panic.

I scrub my hands down my face. "You can do this. You've done this so many times. This is no different than any other event you've ever done. Sign a few books. Say hi. Make yourself approachable." I nod. "You got this."

I get out of the car before I can change my mind and rush into the venue looking for my contact. I haven't met him, but he seemed nice on the phone.

I make the mistake of looking at the door. I can see the throngs of people waiting to get in. Just like that, all of the things I had just done to calm down are useless. I can feel my heart rate pick up.

"Mariah?"

I jump slightly at the deep voice behind me as I spin around. My heart is in my mouth. "Y-yes?"

The older-looking gentleman sticks out his hand. "I'm Trevor."

I shakily take his hand and swallow my outrageously beating heart. I shake his hand, giving it a gentle squeeze. "Hi. Pleased to meet you in person." I give him a shaky smile. There's only one thing on my mind right now. "Security? Did we work that out?"

"Yes, ma'am. We have two people who will be working security for you today. They were hired from a local security firm. They're here. They're just walking the grounds."

"And the police department?"

I've only been in Gainesville, Florida, for a few months, and already I'm well-known. I've had to contact the police on more occasions then I care to admit. Not because I get in trouble. Because ever since people realized who I am, they follow me everywhere. I don't get followed by reporters. I don't get followed around by the paparazzi.

No.

It's people. Fans. I love them all, but sometimes their insistence on meeting me and talking to me gets out of control. The need to meet the popular local author. I've always come off as this confident woman. I have no shame in the romance novels I publish, or the sex scenes I write. My social media presence is large. I talk to everyone who reaches out to me.

Which is why I am here. In this situation. Hundreds of fans waiting to meet me. Waiting for me to autograph their books. Take pictures with them. Talk to them. Shake their hands. I don't mind any of that. I never have. It's when they start to get disrespectful. Touchy feely.

"The police are on standby, Ms. Carter."

I nod, but I'm uneasy instantaneously at his words. I want them here. Around. I'd even pay to have one standing next to me. Not that I don't trust the security firm he hired. I trust that they do their best. But I also know they aren't prepared for what's about to happen.

Maybe I need to look into hiring my own private security. I just never expected the level of success I have right now. Everyone wants a piece of me. Mariah Marie. Bestselling author. No one really cares about the girl behind the books. That Mariah Marie is Mariah Carter. Real girl. Real anxiety. Really doesn't like being felt up and treated like an animal in a petting zoo.

I squeeze my eyes shut and follow Trevor around the room as he explains how people will be let in and allowed to mingle. Snacks and beverages have all been set out. My table is set up with all of my marketing materials and paperback copies of my newest book. Security will be standing on either side of me. Trevor will be around to make sure I have everything I need, including drinks.

I try to avoid the door when I open my eyes after a couple of seconds, but it doesn't work. My gaze drifts. The throngs of people just seem to grow exponentially. I'm amazed each time I see a book sell. But I'm even more shocked at how many people show up to one of my signings and want to meet me.

"Ah. Here they are. Ms. Carter, this is Caleb," Trevor says, pointing to a man who could probably be my father. At least he's well built. I might have a chance if he can move. He points to the other one. Younger at least. Not all that well built. Looks a little like a string bean. Dark hair. Tall. Glasses. I don't doubt anyone could walk right through the guy. Maybe he has special ninja skills or something. "And this is Danny."

My mind is not at ease, but I nod at them both and shake their hands. "I hope you understand what you're getting into here. Have you ever been to one of these events before?"

"We have experience at several events, ma'am. I assure you, you'll be safe," Caleb says. I can hear the reassurance he tries to portray. It's not his fault it's falling on deaf ears.

No point in giving them false hope. "My fans get crazy, Caleb. It won't be long before the crowd gets larger, and they all start rushing the table." I point to the ropes arranged in such a manner to keep crowds calm and organized. "These ropes? They aren't going to do much to keep people away."

Caleb gives me a quiet smile. "We have a plan. If it gets out of hand, we'll get you out, and keep you safe."

I search his eyes and force myself to trust him. I don't have any faith they'll be able to keep the crowd calm. But I do think, hope, they'll at least be able to get me out.

I'm not an idiot.

I know they all think I'm being overly cautious. I'm not a crazy famous person. I'm nowhere near the level of Britney Spears or Arianna Grande.

Fucking hell.

I sit down in the chair they've designated for me and hide my face in my hands for a few moments. I know they don't understand the amount of people I bring in.

Trevor seemed a little shell shocked when I asked him if he could accommodate five hundred people. I saw the venue only advertises for a hundred and fifty guests, but that's only indoors. They have the ability to open this room up so people can stream in and out. I was pleased when he said he could. I fell in love with the Depot when I first moved here. But he still doesn't think that many people will come to this event.

"Are you ready, Ms. Carter?" Trevor asks. Danny and Caleb take their positions next to me. Standing like stoic statues.

I can't help but chuckle. "Yes, Trevor. As I'll ever be."

Trevor makes his way to the door while some of his event staff open the door leading to the outside garden area. I fold my hands neatly on the table in front of me and straighten my back. I sit completely still and make the transformation.

Confident Mariah Marie. Author of bestselling romance novels. The one who writes panty dropping and dick hardening sex scenes. I've been told on more than one occasion, though the information has never been asked for, that my sex scenes have ended in a lot of orgasms for my readers. I take it as a compliment that my scenes are that well-written.

I try to keep my shaking hands at bay as the first excited fans walk in. My eyes widen slightly when I see the line just seems to go on forever, but I hide the surprise. That's not who I need to portray right now. I'm supposed to be used to this. This is all second nature to me.

I keep my eye on the crowd, hyper aware of every movement. I keep Caleb and Danny in my peripheral vision at all times as Trevor explains the process. One person at a time at the table. Stick around. Linger and talk as you have refreshments set out behind my table. The crowd nods and smiles as they bounce on their feet.

And with that, it begins. I watch the crowd like a hawk as the first person comes to the table. A young girl. She can't be more than a teenager. Doubtful she's even eighteen. I'm not stupid. I know those under eighteen years old read my work. But part of me wishes that they wouldn't. That they'd just follow rules. I like rules. They're orderly. Clean.

I blink and look up at her. "Hi!" I say with what I hope is a charming and friendly smile. "What's your name?"

Her smile could light up the room. "Ana!" she squeaks and adorably covers her mouth as her eyes widen. It's people like her who keep me going sometimes.

I chuckle. "Ana. Tell me what your favorite book is."

She smiles even brighter. "Oh gosh! No, I can't choose. I love them all! You're the reason I want to become a writer. I never liked reading until I discovered your books. Now, I take every writing class I can. I even have a creative writing class that's college level!"

"That's amazing. I took a college creative writing course, too, my senior year of high school. I had so much fun with it." I give her a truly genuine smile and glance down at the book in her hand. "Would you like me to sign that?"

"Oh my God! Yes, that would be so great!" She looks at the book, embarrassed. "But it's... not yours. It's one of my favorite children's books. I have all of your books on Kindle Unlimited. I can't afford to get them in paperback." She chews her lip and looks down.

"That's okay. What book is it?"

She blushes. "Little Red Riding Hood."

I smile. "I like that book. But... I have something better." I reach down in one of the boxes near me and pull out my new book. I hear her squeal as I start to sign it and can't help but laugh at her excitement. I hand it to her. "Enjoy, Ana. Keep writing, okay?"

"Yes! Oh my God, for sure!" She looks at me shyly as she hugs the book to her chest. "Um... they said we could ask for pictures?"

"Oh! Right. Of course." I stand and wave her around the table. Danny moves aside as I hand her phone to one of the staff members. "Ready?" I put an arm around her. She turns and hugs me. I stiffen slightly as we both smile at the camera. She checks her phone when it's handed back to her and gathers her things.

"Thank you so much, Mariah! This has been the best day ever."

"You're very welcome, Ana." I watch as she walks away grinning from ear to ear while the next person in line comes up to the table.

"Can I just get these autographed?"

I look up at the older guy standing in front of me. "Yeah, sure. Who should I make them out to?" I open the first of five books.

"I'm sorry. My wife. She was in a wreck. She's okay, but these books are the only thing getting her through some days. I'm pretty tired. I've been with her in the hospital most nights." He smiles weakly. "Unless she kicks me out and says she needs her book boyfriend time."

I laugh. "We all need book boyfriend time. I hope she's doing well in her recovery."

"She's doing very well. Making huge strides. Some days are bad, but she has these books to pull her through. Hopefully, my love gives her a little of that strength, too. Her name is Cassie."

"Cassie. I like that name." I smile softly as I begin the autographs. Cassie's husband begins telling me about the wreck in grave detail, and I feel myself feeling far more pain than I should for someone I've never met. The curse of being an empath. At least that's what I've been told I am. Who really knows?

It's another part of signing books and putting on these types of fan events. They're intimate. People tell me a lot of personal things that eventually just drain me. I know I'll go home tonight and feel exhausted. Far more exhausted than I would normally because I'll take on the emotions of everyone here. All of their stories will play in my mind all day.

I try not to, but it's how it always goes. Part of what makes me the great author everyone believes me to be is not only because I feel all of my characters and their pain. I feel all of my fans, too. It's who I am. I've always been able to deeply feel the emotions of others.

After what seems like hours, I take a chance and look up, hoping the crowd has thinned. But it's truly never-ending. It's like the entire city has come out here today.

I look up at Caleb. "How long has it been?"

"Two hours, ma'am." He looks at the crowd and squints. "Doesn't look like it's letting up."

I sigh. "I need a break. Can you get Trevor over here?"

"Yes, ma'am," he drawls as he signals for Trevor. Trevor hurries to me.

"Ms. Carter. Is everything going well?"

"Oh. Yeah. Everything is fine. I just need a break and some water. It's getting really hot out there." I nod towards the open face of the building. It sort of reminds me of a barn. If I remember when I took the tour of the Depot, though, this was actually where they stored the equipment needed to repair locomotives.

"Of course. I'll have the staff hold the crowd."

"Thank you." I take a picture with the person whose book I just signed and yawn.

I love Florida. I love everyone's Southern accents. I love the weather. The tropical atmosphere. The fact that snow is rare. I *do not* love when the weather decides to be above average. There should be something illegal about weather being in the nineties. Seriously. There should be a way to arrest Mother Nature.

Danny and Caleb lead me to a back room. Danny puts his hand lightly on my lower back as he guides me through the crowd. I wouldn't be upset or uncomfortable with the touch. Except I can feel the slight shake of his hand. How sweaty his palm is. I shiver and inadvertently step closer to Caleb as we walk.

After I've cooled down and grabbed an extra bottle of water, I let them lead me back out into the event area.

As is usual after I take a time out, the crowd has gotten restless. Those who have been waiting for hours for their autograph and picture are getting frustrated. It's gotten warm. People are far more crabby in warmer weather.

I sigh as I sit down. Instead of the happy people who were satisfied with a quick photo and signing, the people coming up now are slamming books down, saying very little, and glaring at me. The friendly smile I had plastered on my face is far more forced.

"You realize how long I've stood out there waiting for you? God. The least you could do is go to the bathroom and get a drink before you come out here." The woman glares at me as she slams her book down. "Ash."

I say nothing as I sign the book. I close it and hand it back to her, forcing that smile. "Thank you," I say quietly.

She blinks at me. "That's it? I don't get a picture with you?"

I look at her incredulously. "I am not taking a picture with you if you're going to be rude to me."

Her mouth drops. She turns to the crowd. "Don't ask for a picture with Miss Perfect. Apparently, that's rude."

"Okay, ma'am. Move on," Danny growls low as he steps forward.

"Are you going to throw me out?" She turns back to the crowd. "Y'all! I'm getting thrown out for asking for a picture!"

My eyes widen as the crowd starts murmuring angrily. "No! That's not -"

"You're a bitch!" Ash screams. Caleb and Danny both grab each of her arms and escort her away, leaving me completely defenseless against the crowd in front of me.

"All she wanted was a pic!" someone yells from the back of the room.

Suddenly, the crowd erupts in angry taunts all directed to me. I watch them with my mouth slightly agape. My eyes dart around wildly. My hands grip the table. I feel like my blood stops flowing as my heart beats out of control. The thunder in my ears becomes deafening. I watch as Trevor tries unsuccessfully to calm the crowd.

"Oh God," I whisper.

I look around frantically for Caleb and Danny. They are nowhere in sight. I shake my head and stand up. I have to be dreaming. I have to be. This doesn't happen to authors. It's not like I'm as famous as Nora Roberts or VC Andrews. Or even Stephen King. My books haven't become movies. My books don't sell out minutes after hitting the shelves. This is insane!

The crowd gets angrier as the seconds pass. I look at them all in almost horrified fascination.

"Just take the picture! Are you too good to take a picture?" someone yells.

"She's too good for us!" someone else yells.

I shake my head. "I never said that!" I squeak.

Where is security? I look for them again. They aren't here. Why aren't they here? I quickly flee to the bathroom and lock myself in. I sit in a corner and cover my ears. Tears fall freely as I close my eyes and make myself as small as possible while pressing myself against the wall.

I have to hire my own security. I can't do this anymore. Maybe I should stop signing all together. Become a recluse. Just write.

No one can hurt me that way. No one can yell and scream and bring on the panic attacks that I've worked so hard to keep at bay.

I shake my head against the memories bubbling to the surface. The memories of *him*. *Him* standing over me and yelling as I fought the panic and cried. *Him* telling me to shut up as I struggled to breathe.

But it's no use. *He's* all I can think about now. All I can see now is *him*.

"Stop it, Mariah."

"Please. Stop." I rock back and forth as I cry and tremble. I gasp for air, but my throat feels like it's closing up.

"Shut up, Mariah."

"I'm sorry. I'm so sorry." I lay my head against the wall and shake as my strangled cries turn into sobs.

The voices in the event room fade completely out. Like they don't exist. All that exists is *him*.

"Stop faking it, Mariah. I know you're faking it."

I shake my head. "No. No. I'm not... Please..." The words fall on deaf ears as the world around me fades. I choke on my sobs. "I'm... sorry..."

Chapter Two

★ DJ ★

"Squad twelve and twenty-seven," one of our dispatchers calls over the radio.

I listen quietly as I turn my squad towards the depot. I should be at Headquarters doing paperwork and working on the budget for my patrol officers, but I've had enough of office duty today. It's nice. Not a day to be inside doing mundane work to keep me busy.

When I took the Captain position, I refused to be one of those guys who sits in his office all damn day. I like being a cop. I've always liked patrol. Responding to calls. Helping people. I like coordinating and managing just as much.

But not today. Today is a day to be out on patrol. Enjoying the Florida weather. Warm, but not too hot. Sunny. Perfect skies. Not a cloud in sight.

"Go ahead," Lyric Sharpe, squad twelve, says.

"Go ahead," Lieutenant Matt Chance, squad twenty-seven, responds.

"Disturbance at the Depot's Event Center. A fan of the author doing a signing there was upset and was escorted out. Incited the crowd on her way. RP says the crowd is chanting for the author to come back and finish her signing after she fled their angry taunts," dispatch says.

"10-4. Do we know if the author is still there?" Matt asks.

"RP says she went to the bathroom and locked herself in. Staff has been trying to get in. They hear crying. We're sending medical, as well. RP says his staff thinks she's having trouble breathing. Someone is getting a key to get in."

"10-4. We're en route," Lyric says.

I pick up my mic. "Squad four to radio."

"Squad four," dispatch responds.

"I'm a block away. Put me on the depot call."

"10-4. I'll put you on."

I look both ways at the intersection and accelerate through it when I see there are no vehicles or people. My engine whirs to life underneath me as I speed the rest of the way to the call. There's only one person I can think of that the author would be.

I've responded to a couple of calls involving crowds and bestselling author Mariah Marie. Sweetest girl I've ever met. But she attracts trouble wherever she goes. Coffee shops. The damn park. I can't help but feel bad for her. I'd hate not being able to sit in my favorite chair in my favorite coffee shop for a few minutes without being hounded by people for my autograph.

I pull up to the depot and get out, immediately hearing the distant sounds of sirens. Judging from the amount of people I can see outside waiting to get in, I'm glad my backup isn't far away. Maybe she has security with her this time that I might be able to command to help with crowd control. She doesn't bring them everywhere she goes, but I hope at an event like this, she'd have someone here with her.

I jog to the side of the building. The yelling and taunting gets louder the closer I get to the event center. When I round the corner into the building, I'm immediately looking for security. All I see is an older guy trying to get the crowd to calm down.

As soon as he spots me, he beelines for me. "Am I glad to see you!"

"Where's her security? Does she have any?" I ask.

"They're by the bathroom door. Straight back."

I nod and quickly walk to the back. "Squad twelve and twenty-seven. When you get here, I need you on the crowd. They're pissed."

"Yes, sir," Lyric says. "Almost there."

"Squad four to radio. Get me two more squads out here," I command. "There are lots of people."

"10-4."

I tune out dispatch as I reach the two security guards. Neither of them look like they give a damn or could do anything to keep anyone safe. I don't know what company they work for, but it's not one I'd ever hire.

"Where's Mariah?" I ask them.

"In there," the younger, cocky as fuck one says to me with a glare. "We can handle her, officer."

He doesn't budge. I have at least four inches on the little fucker. I step forward. "Get. Out. Of. The. Way... Now. Go deal with the crowd, or I will tase you and arrest you for non-compliance. Security license will be revoked, and you'll never get hired for another company. Ever."

The older guy grabs his arm and pulls him aside. "Danny. Police take over our scenes. You know that."

"She's our client," Danny growls.

"Move!" I demand as I damn near walk through him. I reach for the door handle as I put my ear to the door. I hear nothing, and it's still locked. "Where's the staff member who has the key?"

"Here! I'm here!" a young girl dressed all in black says as she runs towards me. I step back so she can unlock the door. Her hands shake violently as she cries. I can tell she's scared.

"Let me help," I say softly, reaching for her hand.

"It's okay..." The key breaks. Her eyes widen as she whimpers and looks up at me about ready to start sobbing.

I step to the door again. I knock. "Mariah? Can you hear me? It's Captain Rens." I hear nothing but sobs on the other side of the door. "Mariah, I know you can hear me. I need you to unlock the door. Let me in."

"D-D-D-J?" she cries as she coughs.

"Yes, Mariah. It's me. Come unlock the door." It takes a couple minutes, but I hear the door handle start to jiggle. "Good girl. Unlock it for me."

"C-Can't…" She's gasping for air. I can hear her clawing the door. Panicking.

"Mariah. It's okay. I'll get you out. Do you trust me?"

"Y-yes…" she sobs as she wheezes. She's hyperventilating.

"Get back from the door. Go to the farthest wall. I'm going to kick it in." I look up as Matt comes jogging down the hall.

"Lyric has the crowd. Other officers showed up," he says before I have a chance to ask him why he's not dealing with the crowd like I told him to.

I nod. "We're kicking in the door. Mariah? Are you away from the door?"

"Y-yes. Get me out. P-please!" she squeaks.

Matt looks at me as we back up. "She's panicking. Sounds like she's hyperventilating."

"Yeah. Last time I responded to a call involving her she was focusing on breathing and not panicking. Said she has anxiety. Three. Two. One. Kick!" We both launch at the door and bust it down. Mariah is curled in a ball on the floor in damn near fetal position sobbing.

"Shit…," Matt breathes. "Twenty seven to radio. ETA on medical?"

I immediately drop to my knees next to Mariah, letting Matt handle everything else. I barely touch her, but she jumps, curling into herself more. "Mariah," I say quietly. "Mariah it's, DJ. Look at me."

She shakily turns and looks at me, looking like a wild animal who may dart at too sudden of a movement. I fight every instinct I have to take her in my arms.

This is a different Mariah from the one I first met. That Mariah nearly clung to me. Didn't want to let me go even after she was safe.

This Mariah looks terrified that I'm even in the room with her. That I'm close to her. She doesn't just look scared. She looks afraid of me.

I stay kneeling next to her but move back a couple of feet. "Mariah. You know me. You know I'm not going to hurt you. You trusted me before. You trusted me just a second ago. You know you can trust me now. I'll keep you safe."

She blinks at me and looks right through me. Almost like she doesn't see me at all. "DJ…"

"Lyric, get in here," Matt says over the radio. I don't know what he sees that I don't, but I trust my partner.

I don't take my eyes off Mariah. "It's DJ, Mariah. Remember? I helped out a few days ago. I gave you my number."

"I…" She blinks a few times and shakes her head before squeezing her eyes shut. "DJ…"

I turn when I hear Lyric come in. "I don't know what's happening," I say to Lyric as I start to get up.

Lyric's eyes widen. She shakes her head. "No," she says quietly. "Talk to her."

I look at both of them like they're crazy as they start to back out of the room slowly. "The fuck?"

"Trust me," Lyric whispers as she and Matt disappear around the corner.

I don't have the foggiest idea what she's asking of me, but I turn back to Mariah. "I think she's gone crazy." I give her a gentle smile. "But that doesn't shock me much. They say you have to be a little crazy to be a cop."

"M-my dad says that." She gulps in several lungsful of air as she watches me.

I smile. "I don't know what possessed me to become a cop. I was perfectly content being in the Army. I think it had a lot to do with finding my own place in the world and not having to fly all over the place to help people."

"A-Army?" She rubs her chest.

"Yeah. I was an Army Ranger. Funny thing is, I never got out after GPD hired me. I was addicted to the rush I got from going on missions. Saving the world from bad people. Then coming home and saving my city from dangerous criminals."

She slowly sits up, closing her eyes. She keeps rubbing her chest as she takes deeper breaths. She opens her eyes again and looks up at me. The wild, animal-like expressions she had a few minutes ago are slowly fading.

I chance moving a little closer. I don't want to scare her. I still haven't figured out exactly what's happening. I've seen panic attacks. I know she gets them. She told me the last time I saw her. It's the reason I gave her my number.

Part of it anyway. The other part is that I can't deny how beautiful she is, and how I'm attracted to her. I've wracked my brain ever since I first saw her, but I can't come up with what exactly it is about her that's so different from anyone I've ever been with. Something that draws me to her, and makes me not want to be away from her. Something that makes me think of her even when I shouldn't be.

"Feeling better? What can I do for you?" I ask as calmly as I can.

She sits up a little more and props herself against the wall. "Not think I'm crazy?" She smiles weakly and speaks softly as she continues rubbing her chest.

I grin. "I don't think you're crazy. I am curious about you, though."

She shakes her head slowly as she looks down. "Don't be. I'm not that interesting."

"Actually, I think you're pretty damn interesting." I get a little closer to her when I hear the paramedics arrive. Her eyes dart over my shoulder. "Mariah. No. Eyes on me. Look at me." I don't look away from her. She does as she's told. "They called the paramedics. They could hear you choking in here. Like you couldn't breathe. But it looks like you're starting to calm down. So if you want me to send them away, I will. You tell me what you need."

She watches me. "I…" She shakes her head slowly. "I don't need them… I'm coming down."

"Okay." I start to get up, but her small hand shoots out and grips my belt near my gun.

She pulls me back down. "Please don't leave me. It's stupid, but you're calming me."

"It's not stupid. I don't know what happened in your life to make you feel like it's stupid, but it isn't, honey. I don't mind being the one to help you."

"Paramedics good to come in, Cap?" Matt asks over the radio.

I look at Mariah. "She said she doesn't need them," I say over the radio, silently thanking both him and Lyric for keeping them away. I have no doubts that more people in this room would set her off again.

She smiles softly. "Thank you," she whispers. "I can't handle more people. I just want to go home."

"Then I'll take you home. As long as you don't mind me hanging around making sure you're okay."

"You have to work… Don't be silly. I'll be okay."

"I can see how strong you are. But I wasn't giving you an option. I want to make sure you're okay. So if home is where you want to go, then home is where you'll go. But I'm not leaving you alone until I know you're okay."

She looks at me for a long moment before she finally nods. "Okay… But…" She looks regretfully at the crowd. "I have autographs I need to finish."

I shake my head. "Not a chance in hell. I'll have my officers hand out books if you have them, but I won't let you continue. And they don't deserve it anyway. Not after what I walked in on. They were screaming and chanting and taunting you, Mariah. No."

She shakes her head. "I can't just let them all leave with nothing. That's not who I am." She starts to get up. "I have to finish." Her eyes dart again to the door. "But maybe I can pay the police department to stay? The security I hired is worthless." She scrubs her hands down her face as I stand next to her.

I reach out and tentatively take her arm. "You don't have to do this. I'll escort you out of here."

"Not all of them are bad, DJ." She looks down at the floor. "I just need to be better about fighting through my anxiety."

"Mariah. Come on." I look at her incredulously. "You -"

She looks up at me as she puts a hand against my chest and smiles softly. "They got me where I am. I owe them something."

"Then, I'm staying. I'll pull Matt and Lyric from patrol to help, but I'm not letting you go out there alone."

She looks at me for a few seconds as her hand slides down my chest to her side. "I know I'm supposed to pay for you to do that. I grew up around cops. I know the deal."

"I don't care. Let me deal with that. If you really want to go back out there I won't stop you. Just know that I strongly advise against it, and that I'm not leaving your side. Your sham of security goes home. I run this my way. I say we leave, then we leave."

"Okay. Deal."

"And you tell me later what caused this. Because I've seen you panicking in crowds before, but I've never seen you scared shitless on the ground like that. Especially when seconds before you were okay enough to know who I was. Then, when I got through that door, you looked right through me and were scared to death."

She bites her lip and hugs herself. "It's not that interesting of a story." She shrugs. "I just suffer from anxiety. And panic."

"Mariah, there's anxiety and panic… Then there's that." I gesture to the ground and fight myself not to hug her. Why I feel so protective of this girl is something I don't know that I understand. It's never happened before. I'm protective of my city. But with her?

I mentally kick myself. I'm not the type of man who believes in relationships. I've had a couple. They didn't work out. I decided a long time ago that I'm much better off on my own.

So, why I can't get her out of my head or walk away from her is something that doesn't make sense. I don't understand why I'm far more protective of her than I've ever been over anyone in my life. I barely know this girl and already all I want to do is just be near her making sure she's safe.

I shake my head and turn, leading her out of the bathroom. Matt and Lyric are both leaning against the wall. I take Mariah's hand when I feel her inch closer to me. I don't know why I'm able to feel her anxiety right now, or why I'm so intune to her, but it's an internal battle for another day.

Mariah tightens her grip on my hand and leans into my back when I stop in front of Matt. Keeping her safe. Getting her through this. That's the priority.

Matt looks at me. "What's the plan, Cap?"

I love that he knows he's not leaving. I also love that he's fucking with me. I hate being called 'Cap,' but he does it when he knows he needs to calm me down. Just him joking with me is sometimes all I need to regroup.

Matt isn't my long time best friend for nothing. The guy can read me like no other. He's the only person I've ever let get close to me. I'm close to fifty, but he's the only family I have left. I don't have siblings and lost both of my parents many years ago. It's always been easier to keep people at arm's length. Less drama. Simpler life.

Lyric smiles and quietly stands next to Matt. She is truly dwarfed by his size. He looks massive compared to her. His arms are covered in tattoos. His short, brown hair and coffee colored eyes fit his dark and commanding personality to a tee.

She's small, with shoulder length brown hair and large tits that don't fit with the rest of her body. I'm not proud I've noticed considering ever since she walked into this department, she's been Matt's. And he's been just as much hers. He hasn't looked at another woman ever since he laid eyes on his hazel-eyed British beauty.

I was damn proud to be his best man when he married her. She suits him. She doesn't let him get away with anything, and he keeps her brat side under control. It's a love I've strived for but never found and gave up on.

Yet somehow, here I am. Internally wishing that maybe Mariah might give me an eventual chance. Completely unlike me. At least the me I am now. Maybe not the me ten years ago when I was still relatively young, and probably a little stupid.

I mentally slap myself and force myself to focus. I squeeze Mariah's hand as I look at Matt. "She wants to finish the autographs. I can't say I fully understand why, but it's important to her."

"She wants to make sure the non-asshole fans get what they came here for," Lyric says quietly. She smiles at Mariah when Mariah peeks out from behind my back.

"Exactly," Mariah says shyly. "I don't want to punish all for the actions of a few."

Matt grins the grin reserved only for the women he likes. Slightly flirty. Mostly friendly. All charm. He gives Mariah a wink. "Then let's get you out there. DJ can stand next to you. Lyric and I will be near. We'll have any instigators thrown out."

Mariah nods and tightens her grip on my hand. "Wh-Where's Danny? And Caleb?"

"I put them on crowd control. If we need to remove someone, I'll have them remove them so Lyric and I will still be near," Matt says as he gives her another smile and nudges Lyric ahead of him.

I turn back to Mariah and take her other hand. She looks up at me shyly. I can't help the smile that spreads across my face. "You haven't met him. But that's Matt Chance. He's a Lieutenant. The woman is Lyric. She's his wife. Also one of the best cops I have working under me."

She nods as she takes a deep breath. "Thank you. For… everything."

I let go of one of her hands and push her hair behind her ear, not able to resist the temptation of feeling her silky strands beneath my fingertips. When the subtle scent of her coconut shampoo hits me, I regret nothing and damn near kiss her.

Instead, I pull back, with great effort, and lead her out to face the crowd. Fuck if anyone thinks they're going to say a hurtful thing to her, though. One wrong word, and I might arrest everyone. Anything it takes to keep that beautiful, soft smile on her face.

The joy signing those autographs and talking to some of her fans brings is all I need to understand why she does this. Why she puts herself through it and takes everything hurled at her. It's the connection to them. I realize I don't mind being the barrier between her and them. If it means she's able to make that connection with those that respect her and admire her, I'm happy to help.

I also enjoy the time I get to be near her. I really just need to get off my ass and do something about these feelings I'm suddenly inundated with. Because this ridiculous infatuation I have with the girl is starting to affect my entire life. I can't concentrate on anything without her popping in my mind.

She's intriguing. Mysterious. Beautiful. Her strength is astounding. Her tenacity is mind-blowing at best. I can see a little bit of the woman underneath the facade. All I can think of is uncovering every single one of her complex layers until she's completely bared for me. I haven't said it, or even thought it, in a long time, but I want her. I want all of her. I want her to be mine.

The only problem is I don't know if I can go through another heartbreak. I don't think I'd be able to come out of it and piece myself back together this time.

Maybe it's best for me to stay on the sidelines. One step behind her. Like a guardian angel or some shit. Protecting my heart from being shattered is almost as important to me as the feelings I'm fighting for her.

Almost.

Chapter Three

☆ Mariah ☆

I close my bedroom door and lean against it. I let out a long breath and close my eyes. Going outside is exhausting for me. Completely fucking exhausting. It's not because everywhere I go I seem to attract attention. I don't understand how I became so recognizable since I moved here to Gainesville, but for some reason… it happened.

I'm fairly certain it has a lot to do with the fact that I've started to really put myself out there. I only moved here a few months ago. But already I've done six signings. One of my goals when I left Duluth, Minnesota, was to truly make something of myself. No one to hold me back. No one to say I can't. No one to ask me if I got a job yet.

I sigh as I walk to my dresser. I pull out shorts and a tank top and walk to the bathroom to clean up and change. I love Gainesville so much, but sometimes the heat gets to me as much as simply being outside does. I hate sweating. Almost as much as I don't like being around people.

A person is fine. Talking to one person at a time in a controlled setting. I have no problem with that. But when there's a lot of people around, I get itchy. My pulse picks up. I can think of nothing more than getting out.

And that is one of the reasons I've forced myself to do book signings. It's a way for me to combat the anxiety. Anxiety I fought so hard to fight in the first place. And I really was doing so well.

I sniffle and shake my head to rid myself of the images. I won't think of *him*. I won't. He's already gotten enough of my tears. Tears that he isn't worth.

I walk out of the bedroom quietly and smile softly when I see him. DJ. Ever since the first day I saw him, I haven't been able to stop thinking about him. It was just after my first signing. I'd gone to Subway to pick up a salad for dinner. Someone from the signing was there. She had a few of her friends. Before I knew what was happening, all six of them were swarming me.

I had a few extra books. I signed them and gave them to her friends, but that didn't seem to stop them from crowding me. I tried to shake it off and just talk to them; play to them. But it didn't really work out that well for me. They wouldn't let me even order. They were all shooting questions at me one right after another.

Somehow, the young girl behind the counter must have seen my discomfort. She told them all to go sit down. They didn't listen. So she called the police. DJ was the officer who showed up.

He also showed up the very next day when all I was trying to do was get a coffee. Though that time, I'm not convinced he wasn't already there and just walked in to get a coffee or something. This girl behind the counter recognized me and was upset about a scene I wrote. She started telling me I was a terrible writer and should stop.

My mind automatically went to everyone in Duluth who told me I couldn't do it. I sucked. I'll never make it. I nearly ran into DJ with my coffee in my haste to get out. I don't know what he said to her after I left, but before I did, DJ took me outside and calmed me down. Got me out of my head. Joked around with me.

I smile when I think of how easily he shut off that switch in my mind before I started panicking. Truly panicking. How he brought me back before I got there. No one has been able to do that for me before. Not that anyone had ever really tried.

DJ turns to me holding one of my books in his hand. He smiles when he sees me watching him. "I've never read a romance book." He flips through the pages and whistles. "But damn. You have a way with words."

I laugh quietly. "Better than porn, they say."

DJ raises an eyebrow then laughs as he nods and closes the book. "I wasn't going to say that. But yes. Better than porn." He turns back to my bookshelf. I don't miss his subtle adjustment of himself.

If I'm being honest, DJ is truly a beautiful man. He's tall. He probably has a foot on my five feet three inches. Even underneath the bulkiness of his bulletproof vest and all of the equipment he wears with his uniform, I can tell he takes care of himself. He probably spends a lot of time perfecting that body.

His eyes are a piercing jade green that could probably penetrate all of the protective barriers I've built around me if I let them. His hair is still dark, as is the scruff on his face, but I can see a little bit of lighter color in it. If I look closely I can see there's slight crow's feet near his eyes. And when he smiles, I can see a few more lines.

He's perfect. He's absolutely perfect. So perfect that I'm sure he has women bowing down at his feet just to bask in his presence on a daily basis.

I bite my lip as I turn away and head for the refrigerator. I have no business thinking about him like that. I could never even dream of being in the same class as him. I've never been able to snag a man like him.

Not for lack of trying. I'm just not pretty enough. I've never been good enough. I gave up hope long ago that I'd ever end up in a truly happy relationship with anyone other than myself. I may be my own worst critic, but at least I know how to get myself off and not bring myself down every single day of my life.

I have my moments. There are days I wake up and bash myself to no extent about all of my imperfections. But when it all comes down to it, I feel like I'm realistic. Women with big tits that are disproportionate to her body, hips that are wide, and an ass that isn't a tiny little thing don't get guys like Captain DJ Rens.

It doesn't matter how attractive he is, or how hopelessly intrigued with him I am. I know better than to hope for a guy like him to notice me for anything more than my crazy psychological state. Or the drama I bring with me wherever I seem to go.

I do believe I'm beautiful. I'm just not the type of woman who is afraid to eat. I've lost a lot of weight over the past few years. I'm happy where I am. Still not the supermodel type of woman typically seen with guys like DJ.

I grab a water and turn to see DJ staring intensely at me. I shiver. And not at all because I'm cold. The look sends an intense, very wet warmth between my thighs that has never happened by a look given to me by a man before. I cross my legs as I lean on the bar. If a look can bring me to a damn near orgasm, I wonder what he could do if he were actually trying.

I clear my throat and curse myself for the ridiculous thought. "Um… Would you like some water?"

"I'd love one. Thank you." He walks so self-assuredly towards the bar separating my kitchen and living room, I nearly laugh. It dies on my tongue, though. Because there's nothing funny about how sexy he looks in that uniform. Or how when he walks I can literally see his muscles rippling.

I turn back to the refrigerator and grab another water. He sits on a stool on the other side of the bar. I smile as I hand him the bottle. I lean down on the bar again and focus on my bottle. Looking at him is doing… things. Things that will help me out later tonight, but that needs to be ignored right now.

"So? What happened today?"

I nearly choke on the sip of water I just swallowed. I guess I should have known better, but I really thought that maybe he had completely forgotten about the reason he's sitting here in my apartment.

I sigh as I look at him. "I… really just don't want to talk about it…"

He meets my eyes. "I know that you and I aren't best friends, Rih, but after today? I really think you owe me something."

"I don't owe anyone anything, DJ. Not anymore." I shiver slightly at his made up nickname. I've never been called anything like that before. Simple, but sweet. But most of all? It's a play off my name. It's still my name. Not Box. Not some other sexual based nickname or an animal. Me. My name.

I stand and walk to my favorite white chair. It's oversized. It's perfect to curl into and write. Or just tune out the entire world.

I hear DJ sigh heavily. My statement wasn't fair. I instantly regret it, but I also spent my entire life feeling like I owed something to someone.

After I got married, I felt like I owed *him* my entire life. All of me. So much so that somewhere along the way, I lost myself. I don't want to lose myself again. Not for anyone or anything. I won't.

DJ turns towards me and stands with his water bottle. "Mariah, I know that you don't owe me anything. I guess that was the wrong choice of words. I'm just asking you for an explanation. I didn't particularly enjoy kicking open that door and seeing you like that on the floor. I've seen panic attacks. Hell, I've seen you panic." He stands and slowly makes his way towards me. I watch his every movement. He puts his water bottle on the end table next to my chair and kneels in front of me. "But not like that."

I look down at him. I was surprised when he insisted on following me home. I was astounded when he insisted on coming up to my apartment to make sure I got settled and was okay. But the thing that floors me is him right now. Kneeling in front of me. Looking up at me with a look that I'm not prepared for. A look I'm not used to.

Concern.

Real concern.

And... I tilt my head just a little and furrow my brows. Something else. Maybe genuineness? Something more than just the concern a cop might have for some random person he's helping.

"I..." I look down at my hands and play with the Dasani label on my bottle.

"Please, Mariah. I'm having a hard time here seeing someone I actually care about going through some battle that I can't understand."

My eyes snap to his. "C-care for?" Those words. Some of the few words I've always wanted to hear and believe. I've never dared to hope that someone would say them, and actually make me believe them. But looking at him... I can almost believe he means it.

Can he?

He shakes his head slightly as his eyes fill with both pain and heartbreak. "I've been through a lot of shit, but whatever you went through must have been really bad for you to be that surprised that someone cares about you."

I blink at him a few times. "I've never talked about it..."

"I'm not asking for your entire life story. But I want to know what was so bad about today. You were scared. You went from being lucid enough to obey my command to open the door and back away when you couldn't so I could get in. But then it was like you didn't know me and were seeing someone else when I got in. My mind is going wild with scenarios. I don't like any of them."

I take a deep breath before looking down again. "Why?" I ask quietly. "Why do you care? Why are you here with me? Not working like you're supposed to be?"

"Because I'm drawn to you. Because no matter how stupidly cliche it sounds, I couldn't walk away from you even if I wanted to. I haven't liked anyone the way I do you. I'm fighting feelings that I've never felt for anyone. And I don't know how to deal with that right now. What I do know how to deal with, though, is issues. Problems. I know I might not be able to fix it, but I can at least listen. And understand."

I watch him for a few moments. "All I've ever wanted is for someone to listen. Genuinely listen. And care…"

He stands and holds out a hand. I watch him a few more moments, trying to decide if he's real. I haven't opened up to anyone in so long I'm not really even sure I know how to anymore. I don't know why I feel like I can with him.

I shakily take his hand and put my water on the end table next to his. He gently pulls me up. Instead of leading me to the couch, though, like I expect, he doesn't let go of my hand and sits in my chair. No one sits in my chair. Not that I've ever had anyone in my apartment since I moved in, but it's my chair. My safeplace.

What's even more bizarre is I'd probably be pissed if anyone else sat here. So, why am I okay with him?

He tugs me into his lap and casually hugs me to him. Like his arms so softly, yet intimately, around my waist is second nature. Like he does it every day.

Despite my fear, I can't help but melt into him. I lay my head on his shoulder shifting slightly so his gun isn't digging into my hip. I find myself burrowing before I can stop it. Getting far too comfortable with him before I even have the chance to know him.

But as I close my eyes and breathe in that amazingly fresh, earthy scent, and allowing myself to lightly grip his shirt, all of those thoughts fade away. I want to open up to him. Maybe it's because I haven't opened up to anyone for so long. Or maybe it's just him. I find myself slowly trusting him.

His arm falls across my lap while the other grips my hip. I almost cry. The gesture is so sweet and unlike what I'm used to. It feels so good that all I want to do is savor it. I don't want the moment to end.

I grip his shirt tighter, giving up the fight to keep him at the same distance I've kept so many since I left Duluth. "I used to be married," I whisper. "It… wasn't a good marriage."

He rests his chin on my head and grips my hip a little tighter. "I was married a few times. Three actually. None were good. Biggest reason I've been single for the last few years."

I look up at him. "I never would have guessed you were single," I say with a soft smile. "I thought women would be lining up to be in your bed."

He gives me a teasing and super cocky smile. "I didn't say I lacked nightly partners."

I laugh despite myself. "So…, you're Gainesville's playboy?"

He laughs in return. I love the way it sounds. The way it makes my heart flutter. "I wouldn't go that far. But I'm not really all that proud to admit that I've taken a few home just for the release. You know…" He taps my hip with another teasing smile. "When my hand didn't cut it."

I laugh again and shake my head before dropping it back on his shoulder. "I have anxiety. Which you know."

"I do."

"With panic attacks."

"Mmhmm."

I sigh. "It came on in my teens. There were a lot of things. I was molested when I was a kid."

I feel him suck in a breath as his grip tightens. "Fuck…"

"It's okay. I'm okay now. I've even spoken about it at PTSD training for the police. But that's probably a little of when it started. After being molested I mean. The panic and anxiety. I've always been a little… I don't know. Uncomfortable around people. My heart would race. I would just want to hide. I was like seven when I was molested. I didn't know what it was. I thought it was normal. And then the anxiety and panic crept in. I just thought I was crazy. I dealt with it for the most part because I didn't really have another choice."

"Jesus."

"I was okay, for the most part, until my dad started doing things like pulling me out of school. Because he thought there was going to be a school shooting at my high school. The first time he did it, I made it through. I went back my sophomore year. I made it up. I was still going to graduate on time. But he did it again at the end of my junior year. Same reason."

"Why? I mean I get being protective and shit, but pulling you out twice because of a belief? Ruining your chances of graduating on time?"

"He's bi-polar, paranoid, delusional, and schizophrenic. I don't think that last part is diagnosed. He just… got a hair up his ass, I guess. After that, he moved us to a town of four hundred people. But it was on the outskirts of town. There was one person my age in the whole area, and she was almost a mile away. So I had to walk or bike to her house. After my bike broke, he refused to help me fix it. So, I walked. But the isolation was not good for someone who was already prone to anxiety. If it was anyone other than me and her or one of my dad's friends that I was close to, I started having problems. I really didn't like being around a lot of people. But there were a lot of other things going on, as well. With my dad and his mental health."

"Deteriorating?"

"Yeah… kind of. There were forest fires all around us. Like the backside of the mountain we lived near. There was one on the other side of the highway about a mile away from us. There was one in Idaho. There was one on the other side of town across the highway. We were surrounded. The fire chief actually told us that if the fire jumped the highway we would have to get out quickly. We had the car packed with essential things."

"Holy shit. That would cause anxiety for anyone."

"The first panic attack I had was when the wind was shifting all throughout the day. The smoke from all the fires around us hit from all directions. There was no break. My mind took off. I couldn't breathe. I cried. I thought I was dying. My dad, instead of doing anything to help me, said that it was the government. That they put chemicals in the fires. They started the fires. That the chemicals were what was making me feel like I was. From then on, the panic was almost constant. But the worst? I didn't even really know it was happening. I just felt my chest tighten. I could hardly breathe. One day I was arguing with my dad about curfew. I was late. I sprained my ankle on the way home. I was only a couple of minutes. He freaked out. He slapped me. I woke up in the hospital."

DJ is so quiet for such a long while that I finally look up at him to see if he heard me. He lets out a long breath as he looks down at me. "I don't know what to say."

I smile softly and lay my head back on his shoulder, suddenly beyond exhausted. "I actually did really well after I left Montana. I managed to get it under control on my own. I was doing really well until I got married. And it was probably the last four years of it that was bad. I don't know that it all was. There were some good moments. But something brought on a panic attack. I don't really even remember what it was. All I know is it hadn't happened in a long time." I tighten my grip on his shirt and fall silent.

He hugs me closer to him and leans his cheek against my head. "Tell me."

"I was panicking. And... my... now ex... was yelling at me. It was like my panic attack set off a panic attack in him or something. Like he didn't know how to deal with my panic attack, so he had one of his own. At least that's what I thought. And maybe that's what it was. I tried to calm down, but I couldn't with him yelling at me. I told him calmly that him yelling doesn't help me. But it didn't help. As time went on... he just got worse with them. And I got worse with them. I couldn't fight them off because he made them worse."

DJ puts his arms tightly around me. "I get the panic in the crowds. I get the anxiety. But you were scared, Mariah. Terrified. What happened? What did he do that made it that bad?"

"It's... difficult to explain. But... when I had panic attacks, he would shrug them off. Later on, like within the last year of our relationship, it got worse for me. Like it was when it first started happening. I would do things to calm it, but I couldn't. I couldn't leave the house. He told me it was an excuse. That I was faking. I couldn't take showers because closing my eyes would set my mind into this whole crazy thing of being attacked in the shower by fictional characters. He made fun of me for that. It wasn't until later that a repressed memory came back of the man who molested me attacking me in the shower. But when I told him, he just... didn't seem to care. Or maybe he didn't understand. I really don't know. I just felt like a worthless person. Today… I just kept thinking of him. When he said I'm faking. Or when he stood over me telling me to stop in this snide voice. Like… I'm terrified. And you're telling me to stop? Like I can just… shut it off?"

"Oh, Rih."

"My mind just completely ran away. It was like everyone was him. Like everyone who ever said I couldn't do it. I was trying to make them all stop, but it felt like all of their voices just became his. Telling me to stop. That I'm faking. That I'm not good enough. I'll never make it. I just…," I shrug and breathe in his incredibly calming scent. The scent I'm becoming far more used to then I should be.

DJ hugs me tighter as I yawn. "Sleep, honey."

I want to argue. Tell him I'm okay. I can sleep without him telling me to. But the panic hangover is kicking in. The headache. The exhaustion I felt earlier has stepped into something more like a complete depletion of all energy in every part of my body. I feel sick. Weak. Just like I always do after panicking like that. I hate the feeling. I hate not being able to control the fact that I'm about to pass out.

But I like the feeling of being safe. Secure. A feeling I don't recall ever feeling at any point in my life. Truly and honestly protected.

I'm too tired to feel the fear that my head wants me to. The trepidation that he'll think my admission to him is insanity at its finest.

The terror that he won't be here when I wake up…

Chapter Four

☆ DJ ☆

(Two Days Later)

I throw my pen across the room and start rubbing my temples. The numbers in front of me are all running together. I have no hope of finishing this budget today. I have nothing to work with. All of the department's budget has gone almost entirely to salaries. The little bit that's left has gone to things like squad maintenance and hiring new officers. Training them. Ongoing SWAT training. All important things.

But it doesn't help me get my cops the protective equipment they need. It doesn't help me replace bulletproof vests that need to be. It doesn't help me put my officers through some extra training I'd like to. Our budget leaves me no room to do anything without cutting into the budget for something else.

Maybe if the city would give us a fair fucking number to begin with, this wouldn't be a problem. But we haven't received a fair budget in more years than I can even count. None of us have been being paid fairly for the work we do in years. We're one of the lowest paid departments in the state. I'm pretty damn convinced at this point that we're probably below the national average.

On everything.

I close my eyes and continue rubbing my temples. The headache came out of nowhere. I had no hope of stopping it, but I should have expected it. Everything about this budget and this day has been one fucked up mess after another anyway. Why not add a headache on top of it?

I sigh at the knock on my door. I briefly consider shutting off my lights and pretending I'm not here. But then I wouldn't be the Captain that I am. Instead, I force myself to choke back the growl as my phone rings.

"Come in," I say to the intruder as I pick up the phone. "Captain Rens."

"Captain Rens, this is Olga Sidorov. They connected me to you regarding a fugitive you have in custody. Or had in custody. There's some confusion. I need answers," Olga says through a heavy Russian accent.

I smile and watch as Mariah comes into my office quietly. She's dressed in tiny and very short jean shorts that make me wonder if she'd be okay with me removing them with my teeth. The black tank top she's wearing leaves absolutely nothing to the imagination. The girl is perfect. All of her beautiful curves. She's stunning.

I gesture for her to sit when she hovers by the door. "Ms. Sidorov. I'm happy to help." I turn to my computer and rest the phone between my ear and shoulder as Mariah sits down. "Exactly who are you?"

"I work for the parole department in Chicago. We're missing Gavrie Petrov. He's affiliated with the Russian Mob. He's second in command to Egor Fedorov."

"Okay. Just give me a second, Ms. Sidorov." I look her up quickly through several different databases to see if she's legit. Just to make sure her credentials match who she says she is. "What's your badge number?"

She chuckles. "I appreciate the thoroughness, Captain Rens. It's 80145."

I smile. "Okay. Gavrie Petrov. It looks like we arrested him three days ago. He's in Alachua County Jail being held for the U.S. Marshals." I glance at Mariah. She's looking down at her phone quietly. Olga has gone silent. "Ms. Sidorov?"

"I'm here." She sighs heavily. "I called them. They said he wasn't there."

I raise an eyebrow. "I'm looking at their system right now. Unless it hasn't been updated, he should be there. Who did you speak with?"

"A woman named Barbra."

"I know her. Give me a minute. Let me call her. I'll keep you on the line."

"Thank you, Captain."

I quickly dial the number for the jail and enter Barbra's extension. Thankfully, she picks up. "Barbra, it's Captain Rens. I'm looking for a missing inmate. Gavrie Petrov. He was brought in on a DWI and was being held for the U.S. Marshals. I'm looking at it, and it says you have him, but I have Parole out of Chicago telling me they were told he isn't there."

"I'm sorry. It's been chaotic here today. He was just picked up by I.C.E."

"Oh, thank God," Olga says.

"Is that a good thing? I.C.E. isn't the Marshalls," I say, slightly confused.

"It's what we wanted. I was hoping that my I.C.E. contact got there first," she says relieved. "He's facing some very harsh punishment in Russia. We've been working very closely with them ever since he was arrested. Even though he is a serious flight risk, the Judge here granted bail with a condition of heavily supervised release. He was on house arrest, but he skipped on us. We knew it was going to happen, but still couldn't stop it. We think the Judge was paid off. So we appreciate you catching him."

"Happy to help." After saying my goodbyes, I hang up and turn to Mariah. She smiles at me. "You… are a sight for sore eyes." I lean back in my chair and go back to rubbing my temples. "It's been a fuck of a day."

She stands and walks around my desk. She slips behind my chair and starts rubbing my neck and shoulders. Her fingers work skillfully as she moves up the back of my head and massages my entire scalp before moving back down to my neck and shoulders. She repeats the rhythm and has me damn near purring in seconds.

She giggles. "You have a lot of tension going, Captain."

I laugh. "Yeah, I haven't had a very good day. I wanted to get this budget done today and be done with it, but I have nothing to work with. I need to replace some bulletproof vests for some of my officers. I can't. Don't have enough. We have a smaller budget than I think we ever have." I gesture to the papers in front of me. "I can't pull any from anywhere else.

We're just tapped out. I'm usually good about finding excess funds, but fuck. The city is really screwing us this year."

She keeps rubbing my head. "What about grants?"

"Grants?" I glance at her.

She digs her thumbs just below my shoulder blades. I groan. "Grants. The Department of Homeland Security gives out grants for lots of things. Protective equipment is one of them. I'm sure Gainesville would qualify. You can get them for a lot of different things through the federal government. You can't depend on them every single year, but you can get them to supplement budgets like yours. You can even get training ones if you're doing training on particular things. Like Crisis Intervention or Mental Health."

I look up at her completely amazed. "How do you know all that?"

She smiles. "I had a few close friends who were police officers in Duluth. One of them did the Critical Incident Training. And mental health. He was also an FTO and was on TRT, which is like SWAT here. And another was a K9 officer. So both know a lot about grants and where to get them. I listened."

"I know there's grants out there for a lot of things, but I've never been able to get the department to back me up on them. Maybe now they'll start listening to me." I reach back and take her wrists in my hands. I gently tug her around and pull her into my lap. "So? To what do I owe the pleasure of such a pretty distraction?"

She blushes a beautiful shade of pink and looks down at my hand resting on her thigh. "I wanted to thank you. For the other day. And for not thinking I'm crazy. And still talking to me." She plays with her fingers. "You're the only person I let into my apartment since I moved here. And the only person I've ever really been that open and honest with about things. I... sort of thought you wouldn't ever want to talk to me again, but you've been texting and calling and just being... so nice."

I smile and gently grip her chin between my thumb and finger. I tilt her face so she's looking at me. "There's a lot to like about you. And all of that other shit? I don't think you're crazy. I'd never do any of the things that have been done to you. Never."

She gives me an adorable smile and hugs me. "I have a truly hard time trusting. But thank you. It's really weird. I do trust you and what you say. I feel like I can."

"You can." I hug her a few minutes before pulling away enough to look at her. "So? What smells so delicious? I saw that bag you brought in."

She smiles brightly, and her blue eyes light up. "Well, I know cops get busy and don't get to eat sometimes. Something told me you might need a little nourishment." She gets up and walks to the insulated bag. She pulls out two aluminum tumblers. "I have iced tea." She reaches in and pulls out a lidded plastic bowl. "Potato salad. Homemade. Though…, it's my first attempt at that. I hope you like it."

I smile as I rest my arms on my desk. My stomach growls. "It smells good."

She pulls out another lidded bowl. "And I have fried chicken. I wasn't sure if you'd be okay with cold fried chicken. So I just made it and packed it up in aluminum foil so it stayed warm in the bag." She pulls out a couple of plastic plates and some silverware.

"Damn. You thought of everything."

Her smile widens. "I may have wanted to impress you," she says quietly.

"Well, color me impressed, beautiful."

She blushes again and sits down. She starts dishing out everything as I watch her. We eat in silence a few minutes before she finally speaks.

"Do you think… maybe you'd like to go out? Sometime?" She doesn't look up at me.

I smile as I swallow. "Sure."

Her eyes snap to mine, like she's surprised I said yes. "Really?"

I can't help but laugh. "Yes, Mariah. Really. I think I've made it pretty obvious that I like you. But knowing what you left behind made me a little hesitant to outright ask you."

She smiles softly. "It made me a little hesitant to ask. Actually, I'm a little unsure how I just got so brave and did it."

"I'm glad you did. How about… dinner and a movie?"

"Okay. But maybe you let me make dinner, and we have a movie in?" She looks up at me hesitantly.

"If you cook something like this," I point my fork at my plate. "Then I'm down for that."

She blushes again, but smiles. "Okay."

"How about I come over after work tonight? You tell me what to bring."

She shakes her head. "You don't need to bring anything. I have everything we need."

I chuckle and finish off my lunch. I'm getting a little too used to hearing her voice. I'm really enjoying seeing that blush. And when her name pops up on my phone, it makes my entire day. I hadn't intended on it happening, but the more I talk to her, the more I like her and want to spend time with her.

I can't say I've ever truly felt the need to want to spend time with any other woman I've been with. Enjoy them? Yes. Want them around me all of the time? It's never been like that for me.

It's different with Mariah, though. Not only can I not stop thinking about her, but I also don't want to be away from her.

★★★

Later that night, after I've cleaned up, I find myself completely nervous knocking on Mariah's door. Why, I couldn't say. But I feel like a scared teenager picking up his date for prom. Another feeling I've never felt. Even when I picked up my actual date for prom.

I shake it off and knock on Mariah's door. When she answers, I find myself speechless. Her long dark hair is pulled back and braided. Her pink tank top hugs every single one of her curves instantly making my mouth water. And the jean cutoffs I've come to the conclusion she loves are the perfect length to show off her golden legs and flawless ass.

She smiles that beautiful smile. I almost melt. She crosses her legs and leans against the door as she looks up at me. "Planning on coming in? Or are you going to stare all day at me?"

I grin teasingly. "I think I might stare all day."

She giggles then blushes and covers her mouth as her eyes widen. "I don't giggle."

I laugh. "That was a giggle." I suddenly remember the bouquet of flowers in my hand. "Oh. These are for you. I bought them then realized I don't even know if you like flowers."

She drops her hand and looks at the flowers excitedly. "I love flowers. I'm not a rose fan, though. Unless they're black." She takes the flowers and turns for the kitchen. She finds a vase and puts water in it.

"I like black roses. I don't know why, but I felt like you didn't like roses." I mentally pat myself on the back for trusting my instincts and getting a pretty bouquet of Spring flowers.

"This is a beautiful bouquet." She looks up at me. "No one has ever gotten me a bouquet before."

I shake my head in disbelief. "Never? None of your exes?"

"Nope." She focuses on arranging the flowers in the vase. "I've only been with three people. And of those three people, I've only had sex with two of them. My ex-husband and best friend. You'd think that maybe after that, I'd get a bouquet, but no. He's given me a flower before. But always ones I bought. And never a bouquet. And my best friend, well, he just didn't."

"Hang on." I lean against the counter opposite of her and fold my arms over my chest as I look down at her. "Are you telling me you've only had sex with two people?"

She smiles shyly and shrugs. "Technically two. And I'm not proud to admit that the second was while I was married… But in my defense, my marriage was over long before the paperwork was signed." She looks down, refusing to look at me. "Though, all of that is embarrassing to admit. I'm not a cheater. That's just not who I am. But… he made me feel like I actually mattered. Like I was pretty and desired. And was worth more to him than just a caregiver. Or like a mother figure or something. And by that time, I actually hadn't been intimate with my at the time husband for more than a year."

I nearly choke as my eyes widen. "Jesus. So many questions."

She laughs and looks up at me. "I don't know why I just admitted all of that to you."

I smile. "By all means. Continue."

"You're a really good listener."

"I try. So tell me about this no intimacy thing. And the mother figure shit. Your ex have mommy issues?"

"Not exactly." She fiddles with the flowers then sighs. She leans against the bar in front of me. "He had a lot of issues. A lot. He had heart issues that started when he was like two months old or something. He had heart surgery to close a hole in it, but the area that it was, they couldn't repair it. It was in the seventies so…" She shrugs. "Technology wasn't as advanced. They ended up building a bridge over the hole so the blood flowed over it. Over time, the scar tissue closed the hole. But the surgery itself was hard. They actually cut off oxygen to his brain. It caused an oxygen deprivation. Which caused a mental defect. He has issues learning and remembering and things. And he'll never really be more intelligent than a nineteen-year-old."

"I get it. His brain just basically stops developing. The cognitive portion anyway."

She nods. "So simple things like paying bills and just day to day things… he really couldn't do. I basically ended up being a caregiver. Like controlling the money. Making sure he took his prescriptions. Made doctor appointments. Made sure he got to them. At one point, I was the sole income maker. We were on state aid. If I made more than a certain amount, we were kicked off. And I couldn't afford medical or food or even rent without the state aid. It was truly rough. But I did it because I felt like it was my responsibility. At the time I really thought that I loved him. But things got bad really fast." She falls silent.

I question a moment if I should push her. In the end, I decide to ask. "What do you mean bad?"

She looks down as she takes a deep breath. After a moment she moves to the oven and pulls out some delectable smelling dish. "I hope you don't mind lasagna." She pulls out something from the fridge and puts it in the oven. I don't miss the absolute avoidance of the question.

"I haven't had homemade lasagna in something like forty years." I smile as she looks back at me.

"Good. Hopefully, you'll enjoy it then."

A while later, after dinner, we both settle on the couch. Mariah curls into my side as I put an arm around her. She turns the movie on after she's comfortable. I reach back and pull the fleece off the back of the couch. I throw it over us.

"After that incredible meal, we may as well do the rest of the night right. A movie isn't a movie without a blanket if we're going to be snuggling."

She laughs. "You might be too good to be true, Captain Rens."

I smile as cockily as possible. "You might be right."

She teasingly swats me as the movie starts. "I love this movie. Storm movies or movies about natural disasters are my favorite."

"*A Day After Tomorrow*? I've never seen it."

"Hopefully you like it. It's about a whole climate shift that happens so suddenly that there's no time to prepare. It's really good."

"Hmm. Well, even if I don't like it, I'm still in good company. A beautiful woman in my arms is better than any movie. Good or bad."

Her smile could light up the room. She curls closer and puts her arm around my waist as she sighs in contentment. It's right then that I make it my mission to undo whatever has been done to her in the past.

I've been getting her to open up little by little. My goal is to watch her unravel for me. Piece by piece. And as each bit of her falls at my feet, I'm going to put her back together again.

The right way.

The way she deserves to be put together and has obviously never been.

I plan to show her the way she should be treated.

Cherished.

Loved.

Chapter Five

☆ *Mariah* ☆

(Two Weeks Later)

I sit quietly next to DJ as the Chief of Police of the Gainesville Police Department speaks of the Gainesville Police Foundation and what its purpose is. DJ's friend and coworker, Lyric, is sitting next to me. Her husband, Matt, is next to her. Each are dressed so formally that I feel completely out of my league. But I already like them both. They're incredibly nice and have made me feel like part of their group, even though I am the farthest thing from a police officer like they are.

DJ and Matt are both in black tuxes that show off exactly how sculpted they are. Over the past couple of weeks, all I've seen DJ in is his uniform or jeans and a t-shirt. This very formal attire he's in is incredibly sexy. It also isn't a bad thing that the black slacks and jacket accents every single one of his features and brings out the deep green of his eyes to literal perfection. I'm not the only person in the room who can't keep my eyes off him.

Though, I think the person that has stolen the entire show at this table is Lyric. The pretty lavender dress she's wearing hugs every beautiful curve. The halter top style dress dips low, but not low enough to make her look cheap. The back of the dress is open and dips near her hips. I am not brave enough to wear anything like that, but she looks incredible. Especially with her hair swept on top of her head in a messy bun that doesn't look messy at all.

I can't help but constantly glance down at my very simple sundress. I hate dresses. But when DJ asked me to come to this police charity event for his department, I almost cried. Not because I've never really been asked on a real date. It was because the event is formal. I don't own anything remotely close to formal. In the slightest little bit.

The closest I have is this black sundress. It's a spaghetti strap and hits just above my knee. Since I have large boobs, it always looks like I'm going to spill out of anything I wear. This dress is no different, and I find myself constantly adjusting. I tried shopping for a more formal one but nothing worked. Nothing fit right.

DJ leans over and whispers in my ear as he drops a hand on the back of my chair. His thumb grazes the back of my arm. "You look beautiful."

I smile softly and tug at the bottom of the dress as I lean into him. I keep my voice low as I turn to him. "I feel so out of place. Everyone here looks so glamorous."

He smiles and kisses my temple. He keeps grazing my arm with his thumb like he does it all the time. He's touched me before, but not quite like this. It feels different. I find myself almost melting at the new level of intimacy. It almost relaxes me.

"Stop tugging on it. You look just as glamorous as everyone else." His breath is hot against my ear and sends shivers down my spine.

I cross my legs and squeeze my thighs together. As per usual, just the sound of his voice has my blood singing for him. My physical reaction to him is ridiculous, and something I don't understand. I've never had it for anyone. It's just so intense. All he has to do is look at me. My panties are instantly wet. It's unfair.

I stop tugging on my dress and try to stay still. It's not that easy with how uncomfortable I feel. So out of place. I force it from my mind and scoot closer to DJ. I subtly lean into him and focus on the speech, but it really is no use. I can't keep my mind off everyone's immaculate wardrobe choices.

Finally, the Chief stops talking. Lyric stands and takes my hand, pulling me up with her. I'm so surprised that all I can do is blink.

"We're going to the bathroom to freshen up," Lyric says. She bends gracefully and kisses Matt. "Be back."

I smile at DJ as she tugs me behind her to the restrooms. I love her accent. British accents are sexy on guys, but on a girl? Completely adorable.

Lyric is really rather small. She's around my height. But she's proportioned perfectly to her small bone structure. Except for her tits. She has large ones like me, but hers, much like she is, are just perfect. I'd be jealous as hell if she wasn't so adorable.

I sink against the bathroom door when I close it behind us and take a long deep breath. "Holy God… Thank you for getting me out of there."

She smiles shyly. "I know the signs of a woman who is in her head. Happens to me more often than not." She cocks a hip and leans against the bathroom counter. She tilts her head as she looks at me.

I sigh and walk to the counter. I stand next to her and cross my arms over my chest. "It's just that everything is so formal. Everyone is dressed in beautiful gowns. And I'm…" I gesture to my dress with another sigh.

Lyric giggles. "You look beautiful. The first time we came to this was just after Matt and I started dating. He wore jeans and a t-shirt. He told me to dress casual. That it wasn't a big deal. So I did. I dressed in a pair of shorts and a t-shirt."

My eyes widen. "No…"

She nods. "Yes. I still haven't forgiven him. He'll never live it down."

I can't help but laugh. "I don't think I'd let him off ever for a stunt like that."

"I ended up marrying him anyway." She smiles and blushes slightly. "He may be clueless in the event category, but he's redeemed himself on numerous different occasions." She reaches over and tucks a strand of hair behind my ear. "You really look amazing. And DJ is crazy about you. I can tell."

I blush and look down. "How long have you known him?"

"Oh, I don't know. A few years. Ever since I started with the police department." She turns around and starts fixing her already flawless hair. "You know, I have anxiety, too. With panic attacks. I know it's not easy to adjust to the world with that. Let alone an entirely new world than the one you created for yourself. So…, if you ever need to talk, I'm here, okay?" She smiles her megawatt smile at me through the mirror.

"I suppose you probably had a huge adjustment. Or…" I bite my lip and shake my head as I look at her. "I'm so sorry. I shouldn't have assumed you weren't born here."

"Oh gosh. Don't worry about it. I wasn't. I came from the United Kingdom. Hardest thing I've ever done. When I think of that move and the huge adjustment after, I know I can get through literally anything."

I turn and adjust my own hair. "That's a good way to look at it. Fearless."

"I have my moments. But… I have Matt to pick me up. And DJ. He's a really great friend. I have a very small circle."

"I've been here for six months. Other than DJ, and now you, I haven't really talked to anyone. The only person who has even been in my apartment is DJ. I feel like a recluse sometimes. And then I feel like something is totally wrong with me for actually liking the fact that I don't really have to leave my place that much."

"It's your safe place. There's nothing wrong with enjoying being there. I only know a little about you. Just what DJ has told me. But I feel like maybe you enjoy it so much because it's yours. And…" She shrugs as she turns back towards me. "It's your safe space." She smiles. "We should head back out. They're probably thinking we fell in or something."

I laugh as I follow her out of the bathroom. She weaves her way through the crowd with practiced ease. I try to keep up, but Lyric is surprisingly fast for someone as small as she is.

Just as I think I'm about to make it through the people milling about, I run smack into someone. Hands grab my arms. Nails dig into my skin. I squeak as I look up.

"Are you okay, Ms. Carter?" Danny asks me. His hands are still on my arms. I try to pull away, but he holds me more firmly.

"Danny. Yeah. I'm okay. I'm just…" My eyes flick towards the direction of my table. "Just trying to get to my table."

"Here. Let me take you."

I try to pull away again, uncomfortable and absolutely not wanting to go anywhere with him. He turns, holding my arm tighter, and starts walking in the opposite direction of my table. My heart relocates to my head and pounds as loud as an F-16 fighter jet. I try to scream, but nothing comes out.

"What the fuck are you doing?" a dangerous, rumbling voice says from behind me. Danny immediately lets go as I'm yanked against a solid chest. I'd be scared to death, but I know the voice.

"Matt," I whimper as I collapse against him. He wraps me in his arms.

"I was just bringing her to her table. She looked distressed. I work private security. I've worked with her before."

"I know who you are. Get the fuck away from her before I let my wife deal with you. Wouldn't be a fair fight if I did. She's pretty fucking ruthless." He keeps me close to his side and guides me through the crowd.

I cling to his waist. "Where..." I swallow. "Where's Lyric?"

"She turned around and saw you weren't behind her. She saw that fucker with his hands on you. DJ had just gone out to the car to grab something he left in there. I saw Lyric's expression change and immediately got up. I got to her just as she was doubling back for you. I made her go back to the table because I'm pretty sure she would've broken that fucker's face." He sits me down and turns his chair so he's facing me as he sits. Lyric wraps her arms around me. "What happened?"

I look at Matt shakily and swallow again as I shake my head. "I..." I close my eyes and shrug before slowly opening them. "I don't know. I ran into him. I was focused on following Lyric. I didn't see him. He grabbed my arms to keep me from falling, but he wouldn't let go. I started getting scared. I couldn't get out of his grasp. He started dragging me away from the table." I shiver.

"The fuck?" DJ kneels next to me and takes both of my hands in his. "What happened, honey?"

I say nothing. I turn and bury my face in his neck. I try not to cry, but any adrenaline I had coursing through my veins is gone. I can't stop the tears that fall from my eyes as I cling to him. I focus completely on his arms around me. His fresh scent. Safety. He's my safety.

Lyric stays plastered to me. Matt runs his hand up and down my back. "We need to get her out of here, DJ," Lyric whispers.

"What happened, my girl?" DJ whispers in my ear as he hugs me as close as he can. I shake my head and dig my fingers into his shoulders.

47

I'm so relieved that he's near that I don't even care I'm probably making a scene. A problem to deal with later.

"I just want to go," I plead. "Please."

"Okay. Okay. We'll go."

DJ stands slowly, pulling me with him. He gently takes my hand in his as I open my eyes and look up at him. He gives me a reassuring smile. I focus on him. His hand holding mine. His proximity. His thumb rubbing slow circles around the top of my hand as he pulls me quickly through the crowd.

I vaguely see Lyric and Matt gathering all of our belongings. I can feel them. I can feel their presence surrounding me when we get outside. Matt's spicy cologne. Lyric's soft and subtle vanilla bean scent.

DJ helps me into his car, then turns to Matt. They speak low as Lyric watches me smiling softly. She'll never understand how just that one action works to calm me down even more. I focus on her until DJ is in the car. He takes my hand and entwines my fingers with his. He kisses my palm before holding my hand tightly as he starts to drive.

As he drives, I attempt to sort out what just happened in my head. I've learned over the years that walking through an event step by step helps to unconfuse everything when it all seems too much for me to follow. This all took place so fast that I'm still not totally sure what transpired.

I use DJ to anchor me. I don't think he realizes just how much his touch does for me. How he centers me. How just him being quiet and letting me work through it means the world to me.

"I was with Lyric. I was calm. I was okay. Then Danny appeared. I didn't even see him. I didn't have my eyes down. I was focused on Lyric and getting to the table, but I wasn't that oblivious to my surroundings."

DJ continues to run his thumb over the back of my hand. "Mmhmm…," he says quietly.

I blink a few times and grip him tighter as I focus on the lights, buildings, and cars that we're flying past. "I was instantly nervous. Just… something about him. I tried pulling away. He held me tighter. Like… gripped me harder. It was hurting me." I absently rub my arm with my other hand and close my eyes. "He pulled me away from the direction I was going. Like he was trying to make me go somewhere else." I open my eyes. "I don't understand why he would do that."

"Do you remember the direction he was trying to pull you?"

I look back out the window as we pull into the parking lot of my apartment complex. "Towards the bathrooms. I just came from there. But he said he was taking me to my table. He wouldn't let go of me."

DJ pulls into a parking place. He turns the car off. I grip his hand tighter, suddenly feeling super vulnerable. I look at him wide-eyed and open my mouth to beg him not to leave me here alone, but no words come out.

He leans over and cups my cheek. "Don't. Don't freak out on me. I'd never leave you after that. I still have sweats and a t-shirt here that I left after our last movie night." He kisses my forehead so sweetly I almost melt. "I'm not going to leave you. I know how scared you are."

I let out a relieved breath. "Okay."

DJ pulls slowly away. He kisses my hand before letting it go as we get out of his convertible black Mustang that I'm completely in love with. He immediately locks our hands together as soon as we reach each other after getting out. DJ leads me into the building. He doesn't let go of my hand even after he's closed and locked the door to my apartment behind us. He leads me to the bedroom and grabs some clothes out.

"Why don't you go take a nice, relaxing bath?" He hands me a pair of tight shorts and a tank top. "I'll make something hot to drink. We can watch a movie if you want to. Or just talk."

I look up at him shyly. "Cuddle?"

He smiles and chuckles. "Anything you want, beautiful."

"How are you so perfect?"

He gives me a cocky, teasing smile. "Practice."

I laugh as I head for the bathroom. I quickly clean up. I don't like showers. They are a trigger. For many years I thought it was because of watching the movie *The Ring*. I hadn't realized until just after I moved here that it had more to do with my past.

The man who molested me did it in the shower one day. I'd blocked it out. It came back to me full force one day. I spent an hour crying in the shower until the water turned cold. Part of me was relieved that it was actually caused by something legitimate, though. That I wasn't as crazy as I thought.

I quickly get dressed and walk out to the living room. DJ has changed into a pair of gray sweats and his favorite green Army t-shirt. He looks up at me and holds out a hand. I take it. He pulls me down on the couch and cuddles me into him.

"*SWAT* is On Demand. I have it queued up and ready to go. Hot chocolate is ready. Popcorn is perfect." He smiles down at me as I look up at him.

"Thank you."

His lips are so close that if I wanted to, I could lean up and kiss him. But the truth is, I'm not entirely certain if we're friends or if we might be more than that. We haven't kissed. Besides cuddling on the couch and watching movies, we haven't done more than hold hands. Our first real date was tonight to the charity event.

I've tried to treat this relationship as just a friendship, but Lyric's words stick in my mind. Could he really be crazy about me? Does he want more than friendship? He is being far more affectionate with me than he usually is. And his deep jade eyes look like they are on fire with something I can't decipher.

I watch him as he leans in slowly. His fingers tangle in my hair as his eyes sear into mine. I shakily put my hand on his chest and lean in the rest of the way when he stops. I close my eyes. A small whimper escapes me when his hot lips meet mine.

I inhale sharply. He tugs my hair. I grip his shirt. He deepens the kiss, slipping his tongue into my mouth and teasing mine with his. I quietly moan into the kiss as every part of me becomes alight with a passion and desire I've never felt before. All of my nerve endings buzz. My blood hums.

He pulls away slowly and runs his fingers through my hair. I open my eyes after a few moments, dazed. He smiles and runs a thumb over my lip. He kisses me softly again and pulls me close to him as he starts the movie.

No words are said. They aren't really needed. The kiss told us all we really needed to know. Any doubts I may have had about where we stand are washed away in the tidal wave of emotion washing over me.

No one has ever kissed me like that. No one has ever put so much emotion into the kiss that I have no doubts of the way they feel.

DJ pulls me closer to him. I melt against him, gripping the hem of his shirt as we settle in for the movie.

For the first time in my life I feel happy. Really and truly happy. Safe. Protected. But most of all?

At peace.

Chapter Six

☆ DJ ☆

(One Month Later)

It's been an entire month since I first kissed Mariah. I couldn't be happier with the way things are going between us. I spend almost every night at her apartment. She brings me lunch almost every day. I like to think I'm helping with her anxiety by getting her out of the house. But she's probably helping me more by giving me something to look forward to when my day isn't going the way I want it to.

Mariah has turned out to be everything I've ever wanted in a woman. She understands my job. She listens to me when my day sucks. She'll cuddle with me when she feels like I don't want to talk about it. And most importantly, she doesn't push me away when I do need to talk.

Most people look at me and see a tough cop. Incapable of feeling emotion or something. Like I'm just some impenetrable force that nothing ever bothers. I've been married. It didn't work. I've taken a lot of women on dates that have ended in very pleasurable endings for us both. Then I moved on when I didn't feel a connection. Somehow that gave me a player's reputation.

But by that time, I'd pretty much given up on finding any kind of true love, so I didn't care what any of the badge bunnies that clamored for my attention thought of me. I became pretty content giving the girl I spent the night with everything romantic. As long as she knew the expectations, it seemed to work well for us both. I got to do what I wanted, which was treat someone like the Queen they should be treated like. At least for a night. And they got the one-night-stand with a cop like they always dreamed.

Mariah is different. She has been from day one. I don't think I've ever met a woman that I actually wanted to spend time with. As much of a dick as it makes me sound, not even any of the women I've been in serious relationships with or married. Mariah is worlds above and beyond them. I can't get enough of her. I can't get enough of her company or the time she gives me.

I look at my watch as I pull up to Mariah's apartment building with dinner. I'm hoping I can get her to eat something before she goes to the book signing she has tonight, but I got held up. We're going to have to hurry. I expect her to be starving since she very rarely steps away from her writing for long enough to eat.

What I don't expect when I use the key she gave me to her apartment is her sitting on the floor in the middle of the room looking at a piece of paper completely scared out of her mind. I've learned her signs well.

I close and lock the door, drop dinner on the counter, and kneel in front of her. I pull her close. She clings to me and buries her face in my neck.

"What happened, baby?" I cradle her in my arms. She says nothing, but bursts into tears as she hands me a piece of paper.

Mariah,

In time, you'll be mine. I'll cherish you like I cherish your books. You'll see me like I
see you. My heart is yours.
Our flame is only kindled. Soon it will be a raging blaze of desire. I'll prove to you that I am worthy of your love.
Soon you'll be by my side where you belong. Nothing will part us.

Yours for eternity,

X

"The fuck is that?" I keep an arm around her as I look for an envelope. "Baby, did this come in anything? An envelope? Anything?"

"T-That…" She points to the couch, but stays plastered to me. There's a giant bear sitting on her couch. "I t-thought it was from you!" She sobs harder.

"That's not from me," I whisper. I pull her up as I get up. I keep her tightly in my arms as I move us to the bear. A six foot fucking brown bear. With a top hat and black tie. Who the fuck buys something like that? I'd walk out of my bedroom at night and think it was a person. Shoot first. Protect my home and family. Ask questions later.

I look the bear over as Mariah tightens her grip around my waist. I set the letter next to it and take out my phone, keeping her safely in my arms.

"Why would a-anyone send a l-letter like that?" She shutters and trembles as she cries.

"I don't know, honey. I wish I did." I dial Matt's number, keeping Mariah facing away from the bear and safely in my arms.

"What's up, DJ?" he asks when he answers.

"Can you get to Mariah's? I'll text you the address. Bring Lyric."

"Yeah, we'll head out right now. What's going on?"

"I'll explain when you get here."

"Okay. I just grabbed Lyric. Text me the address." He hangs up.

Keeping my arm securely around Mariah, I bring her to the bedroom and close the door behind me. I don't trust that bear, but I can't look at it until someone is with her. I won't leave her alone.

I sit with her on her bed and lean in, kissing her softly. I push her hair back from her face. It's then that I notice she's only wearing a towel. She's soaked.

"Rih, what happened?" I wrap her back in my arms as she sniffles. The trembling and shivering has nearly subsided, but I keep her close anyway. I run my fingers through her hair and up and down her back.

"I don't know… I was… getting out of the bath. I heard a knock." She sighs. "I thought it was you. I wrapped a towel around myself and hurried to let you in. When I opened it, the bear fell inside. The note was pinned to its chest." She falls quiet. I keep running my fingers through her hair. "I drug it in... I thought it was from you. I thought you were messing with me. I propped it on the couch and read the note." She sniffles again.

I shake my head. "No, my girl. I'd never do that to you. Or write something like that to you."

"I... just don't understand why someone would do that."

"Have you ever gotten anything like this before? Messages? Emails? Texts? Notes? Anything?"

"Um..." She pulls back and looks up at me. "I've had messages, but I just ignore them, usually. But... I don't know. This last one, I didn't delete it like usual. I actually forgot about it completely. There are a few on there." She grabs her phone and pulls up her social media account before handing it to me.

I scroll through, and chills start running up my spine. "Mariah, how long has this been going on? There are four different accounts with the same type of possessive messages."

She shrugs as she looks at her phone. "I told you. I get messages all the time. But... I don't know. These messages have trickled in over the past couple of weeks. I feel like they're the same person... That's why I kept them all. But I think it was the way that first one came off. The tone was... different than the others. And then those other ones started trickling in." She looks up at me. "I was waiting to see if another came in before I was going to be really overly concerned and tell you."

I read the first one out loud. "I love your work, Mariah. It's so refreshing to read real characters in real life situations. And the sex scenes. Damn! It was great to meet you. See you at the next one!" I look at her. "How often do you get readers telling you that your sex scenes are..." I look at the phone again. "Are 'damn.' Honey, I wish you would have shown me that. Especially if you felt uncomfortable about it." I look at the other ones. All sent on different days over the past couple of weeks. "This one talks about a specific sexual scene. This one says he'll see you at the next event and can't wait until his favorite erotic writer signs his book. This one requests a signature on his favorite sex scene."

"I guess I really just wanted to believe that it was someone who really liked my work..."

"This is classic stalker behavior. I'm going to have someone on our tech team track these accounts. My bet is they all come from the same IP address."

She flops dramatically on the bed. "I didn't want to believe that."

I bite my tongue and avoid looking at the hint of pink nipple that's slipped out of the towel. I stand and put her phone in my pocket. I lean down and kiss her, pulling the towel up before I do something I'm not sure she's ready for. She looks down and blushes when I stand.

"Get dressed. Matt and Lyric will be here soon." I kiss her again and leave the room so she can get dressed.

I close the door behind me and lean against the wall next to it with my arms folded over my chest. I glare at the bear. It seems harmless. It's just sitting there innocently.

Smiling.

But there's something off. Call it a cop's instinct. I feel it. It's not just that it's not from me. It's not the note. I don't like any of that. I don't like that my girlfriend has a stalker. It's the bear itself. There's something about the bear that throws me.

Leave out the fact the thing is only three inches shorter than I am. That it's damn near my size in every way imaginable. Leave out that it came from a stalker. It's the bear itself.

I glare a little harder as someone knocks on the door. I walk to it and check through the peephole. I open it when I see Matt and Lyric. I step back, letting them in.

Lyric scoffs at the bear. "Well, that's not creepy in the least bit."

I smile. "Nope. Not at all."

She looks up at me, giving me a disgusted smile. "For the love of fuck, please tell me you didn't buy that for her."

I laugh. "Fuck no. That…" I point to the intruding bear. "That is from a stalker." I hand Matt the note. He holds it so both him and Lyric can read it.

Matt looks at the bear darkly. "Who the fuck buys something like that and thinks it's okay in any relationship? Let alone for someone they've never met?"

"There's a market for it. Some people really love that kind of thing," Lyric says. "I'm not one of them." She looks at me. "Where is Mariah?"

I nod to the bedroom door as it opens. "There."

Lyric immediately hugs her. "I'm so sorry."

Mariah hugs her back. "It's okay. I'm over the panic now. Now, I just want to figure out who sent it and get that thing out of my house."

"Your strength is something to be desired, sweetheart," Matt says.

Mariah blushes as her and Lyric turn towards the bear, arms locked around each other's waists. "Thank you," Mariah says quietly as she sighs. "I just don't understand what's happening. I'm not that popular."

"Honey, you're a bestseller. You spend a lot of time with your fans. You're bound to draw attention," I say. "But I do agree. This is getting out of hand. The crowd you draw is one thing. This is something else entirely." I hand Matt Mariah's phone and let him see the messages.

He scrolls through them. "Oh, fuck yes. Classic stalker." He hands the phone to Lyric when she reaches for it.

"Has anyone checked for cameras in that abomination they call a romantic gesture?" she asks as she reads the messages.

Matt and I look at each other and head straight for the bear. We both kneel in front of it and start searching for any kind of unnatural stitching job that would indicate a camera may have been placed.

"Fuck me," Matt growls. He yanks the bear's head towards me and glares.

"I knew something was off." I grip both sides of the back of the head and rip. The stitching comes apart easily and stuffing goes everywhere. I hear Mariah gasp. She hates messes. I reach into the back of the head and feel the camera. I pull it out. "Son of a bitch." I hold it up for Matt.

"It's recording. It's been recording this entire time." He takes it and turns it over in his hands. I see the red light indicating it's on. It very suddenly flicks off.

"What did you do?" I take it and look for any kind of power switch.

Matt shakes his head. "It's running off a signal. Signal has been cut."

I look up at him slightly horrified. "We need to get tech out here."

"We'll take it to them. They can't do a hell of a lot from here." He holds out his hand. I give it to him as we stand. He pockets it as we both turn. Mariah is very sadly grabbing her keys and a box that she has on her counter.

I raise an eyebrow. "Baby, what are you doing?"

She looks up at me with an almost defeated look in her eyes that breaks my heart. "I have a book signing. I need to head out." She looks longingly at our long ago forgotten about dinner.

"Mariah, like hell. You're not going out to a book signing after we just found out you have a stalker." I look at her in disbelief that she'd even suggest such a thing.

She looks at me with the determination I love about her. "DJ, I'm not going to hide. I've come so far over the past month with my anxiety since I met you. The attacks are less and less. This helps. You all help. I'm not going to take huge strides backwards and hide just because someone has an unhealthy obsession. My life hasn't been threatened."

"He knows where you live!" I flinch slightly when she does. I walk quickly to her side and take her in my arms. She melts as she lets out a breath. "There's no security plan for you, beautiful. I have no way of making sure you're protected. I can be at your side. Matt can be. Lyric can be. But we have no screening set up. We have no security checkpoint. People are just allowed in without screening at all. They're allowed to come up to you, and be close to you. Now that we know you have a stalker, we have to be more cautious."

"He's right, Mariah. We need to figure out how to keep you safe," Matt puts in.

"But she also needs to be able to go out there and meet her fans. This is how she gains readers and markets herself. This is her livelihood. If she isn't going out to these events and putting herself out there, she loses sales." Lyric looks at both me and Matt as I hug Mariah. "We can't just put a halt on how she makes her living. And this is a huge event for her. There's going to be other authors there and models. Photographers."

"All the more reason to stay far fucking away," I say as I grip my girl's hair. But I know she's right. This is the type of event that can give Mariah sales for the entire year.

Matt scrubs his hand down his face. "There is minimal security at this event. We had an overtime signup sheet for patrol. Two cops are there tonight. As well as a private security firm hired by the venue, but it's the same security firm the Depot hired for Mariah when she did her signing there."

I refuse to let go of her even though she tries to pull back. I kiss the top of her head. "I don't know what you guys planned tonight, but I need you."

"DJ, Mariah is our friend. We care about her, too." Lyric's soft voice and declaration ease my mind slightly. "We aren't going to leave her side. We'll be like her own private security. Only better because we care for her."

"Plans change, DJ. If she needs to go, then we'll go. All of us."

I feel Mariah soften even more at Matt's promise. I pull back only enough to look at her. I run my thumb across her lower lip. "You know I don't like this."

She nods. "I know. But Lyric is right. This event can help me bring in my income for the whole year. But... I would never put my safety in harm's way. I... truly trust you all." She meets my eyes. "I know you'll keep me safe, but if you really don't want me to go, I won't."

I take a deep breath. "I don't. I don't want you to go. But I also trust them to help me keep you safe. We aren't leaving your side. For anything. If you need to go to the bathroom, Lyric goes in with you. Me and Matt stay outside the door. If you need anything, me or Matt will get it. But you are not to be out of our sight. For anything."

"I understand. I trust you." She stands on her tiptoes and kisses my jaw because she can't reach any further up. Especially when I tease her and stand taller like I am right now. She smiles and giggles. I lean down and kiss her.

"I'll grab this. What else do you need?" Matt asks as he grabs the box.

"Nothing. I have the other boxes already in my car."

"We're taking my car, Rih." I take her hand as we head for the door. Lyric locks up behind us as we all head outside.

Mariah laughs. "Don't like my car?"

I shake my head. "No. I don't. Something is wrong with that damn thing. You need a new one."

"There isn't anything wrong with my car. It's just upset with you because you're mean to it."

I crack up. "The front end rattles. You can't use your A/C anymore without the engine overheating. Your back window won't open. And at one point, I'm fairly certain I saw blue smoke coming from under the hood. That isn't normal. Your brakes squeak. Your oil leaks. And your rotors are rusted. All of them. And if that wasn't enough, you definitely have a crack in your radiator. Small? Probably. But it's there."

She giggles as she opens her trunk. "Okay. I might need a new car."

"Your tires are bald," Matt chips in with disbelief. "You aren't allowed to drive this fucking thing anymore. I'm having it towed."

Mariah's mouth drops open as Lyric starts laughing. "What a horrible thing to say. I've never called you bald. No wonder my car has a complex. You all hate him."

I raise an eyebrow as we transfer boxes. "Him?"

"Yes. Him. I once had a girl car, and she was a literal pain in my ass. And I mean that. Not only did she constantly break down, but she also had a spring in the driver's seat that was broken. It was positioned right at my asshole. Whenever I hit a bump, I felt like I was being impaled."

We all laugh again as we finish transferring boxes into my car. Once we're all settled in our vehicles, we drive to the Historic Thomas Center. I knew the event would be large, but I wasn't prepared for just how many people would be here. It sets me at unease, but I know Mariah doesn't need that from me.

Matt and I carry all of her books and materials in as Lyric and Mariah set up the booth she's been assigned. By the time we've carried in the last box, they have everything set up. I'll give it to my girl. She's efficient as fuck. Throw Lyric next to her, and the two could probably rule the world with how they work together.

When people start coming in, Matt and I step back. Lyric sits next to her. I look at him. "Why do I get the feeling this is going to end up blowing up in my face?"

Matt gives me a pained smile. "You ain't the only one."

I groan almost silently as I keep an eye on my girl. I don't know who is behind this, but I won't let them get to Mariah. The girl has become my whole life in a fairly short period of time. She deserves the world. I want nothing more than to be the one to give it to her. And if I need to chase away a few dark souls that come after her while I'm at it, then so be it.

Anything for the girl I've fallen so hard for.

Chapter Seven

☆ Mariah ☆

(One Month Later)

I've stared at a blank screen for hours. I've had writer's block before. It's not like I've never had it or know how to handle it. Go for a walk. Read. Workout. Talk to DJ. Call or text Lyric or Matt. Anything but write.

Funnily enough, I've done that. All of it. I've even taken a bubble bath. But I can't seem to get past it. I haven't written a single word of this book today. I don't even know why. I know how I want it to go. I know the flow. I have outlines of the chapters. It's not like I don't have a starting point. I still can't seem to make myself write.

I sigh and walk outside to my balcony. I sit in my oversized and very comfy chair. I stare out over the city and breathe deeply, allowing myself to think of anything other than the book. It doesn't take long for my mind to drift to DJ.

I smile and hug myself as I cuddle into my chair and close my eyes. DJ is the fantasy of every woman. Maybe every guy. In the two months that I've known him, I've realized that he's the guy all romance authors write about.

DJ is possessive and dominant. He's always in control. He knows what he wants and takes it. He's commanding. He's definitely the Alpha of any room. No one questions him when he makes an order.

And what's more is that he manages to do it in a way that is unequivocally kind. He's never a dick. Not unless he has to be. People follow him because they want to. He leads with his heart. He truly cares about his decisions and actions and how they'll affect those that he commands.

The most important, though, is how he is with me. He's so sweet. Caring. He's incredibly loving. He's honest to a fault. He is compassionate and empathic. His humor is the perfect mix of wit and cynicism.

He's incredibly intuitive. He knows exactly what I need without me even saying a word. He has an incredibly kind heart under that tough exterior. He is the most amazing man I have ever met. I can never express how hard and fast I have fallen for that man. I am so grateful he came into my life.

Out of all the women in the world, this incredible man chose me. He sees something in me that no one else does. He sees the woman I want to be. The woman I strive so hard to be. He sees a strength and beauty in me that I'm working hard to see myself.

"What are you doing out here, beautiful girl?"

I jump and look at DJ as he kneels in front of me. I smile and hug him. "I missed you." I bury my face in his neck.

He hugs me tightly and stands, picking me up and carrying me inside. I lock my arms around his neck and my legs around his waist. I kiss his neck as he tightens his grip. He walks to my bedroom and drops me on the bed, but doesn't let go. Reading me as well as he does, he pulls me to his side and hugs me as hard as he can. I melt into his solid chest.

He kisses my forehead. "Missed me? You just saw me this morning."

I nod and breathe in his cologne. Just like that, I'm centered. Totally centered. "I have writer's block," I say quietly. "I'm trying to write a sex scene. I used to be so good at them. But everything I've run through my head today is just crap. It wouldn't get the horniest of anyone off."

He laughs then tugs my hair and looks at me incredulously. "Is that what you go for when you write? How to get horny people off?"

I smile. "No... It's more I just... write. And whatever happens to the reader because of my words is on them. But today? I can't write anything. It all just sounds terrible."

"Hey. Stop. If there's one thing I know about you, it's that what you write isn't terrible. Even on your off days, you write some incredible stuff. It's what you do."

I look up at him. "But I use inspiration in my writing. I haven't had sex in four years." I squeak when I realize what I just said. His eyes widen. He nearly chokes. I cover my mouth. "I didn't mean to say that..."

"You..." He coughs. "You're kidding. You have to be. You haven't had sex in four years?"

I keep my hand over my mouth and shake my head. "No..."

"Jesus fuck." He flops on his back and puts his arm over his eyes. "How is that even possible?"

I slowly put my hand down. "I can literally count how many times I've had sex on two hands. Well, maybe two hands and a foot."

He turns his head and drops his arm as he looks at me. "How many?"

"Well, let's see. I was married for... a little over ten years. At first it was fine, but the sex was never really a part of the marriage. The first couple of years maybe twice a year? After that it was once a year. Then when he got sick, it was no times a year. All in all? Ten with him. Twice with the other person I was with," I whisper.

He scrubs his hands down his face. "My poor girl. How the fuck did you survive?"

I sigh and smile softly. "Honestly... I guess I just never wanted it. When we were dating, he went down on me one time. Just as I was about to come, he stopped. He didn't like the way I tasted. He never really did anything for foreplay because he didn't like the way I smelled."

"Holy shit. Baby, why? Why did you put up with that? That's so fucked up. Do you realize how fucked up that is?"

I look down and lay my head on his chest. "When I got married it was because I was almost thirty. I didn't want to be alone. My family... they were kind of pushing me. I was coming off a hard break up when I met him. He was nice. And at first he seemed to actually really care about what I wanted and needed. Then... I guess maybe he just wasn't as intelligent as I thought. I guess maybe the doctors were right when they said that he'd never really be more developed mentally than a nineteen year old. I got him off all the time. Blowjobs. Hand jobs. But he never did anything for me."

"He never went down on you after that first time? Never fingered you?"

I shake my head. "After the first time, he never went down on me. As for the fingering. He did it a couple of times. But he just jammed them into me and expected me to come. It was hard and fast, but he didn't know where to touch. Even if I guided him. And he only did it for a few seconds. If I didn't come, then that was it."

"Fucking hell. That pisses me off."

Realizing I never told him any of this, I stopped that first night because I didn't want to talk about it, I continue. "After the first couple of years, he started saying things to me that were just hurtful. Like subtle digs at my weight. I used to be so much heavier. He was really unsupportive of me losing it. If I dieted, he'd get mad at what I ate. If I told him I didn't want fast food, he'd get it anyway. If I told him I didn't want soda or extra sugar added to my tea, he'd buy soda or add extra sugar to the tea. He wanted fried, processed, unhealthy food. I couldn't cook healthy because he would complain so much. He'd say things like 'we need to lose weight,' or poke me in the stomach and say things like 'what's that?' Even when I told him it bothered me, he'd still do it. But then he wouldn't do anything to help me lose it."

DJ turns on his side and wraps me in his arms. "Good thing I never met this asshole."

I cuddle into him, wrapping my arm around his waist. "It's over now."

"I don't blame you for not wanting the sex, and it not being a part of the marriage."

I'm quiet for a long while as I close my eyes. He holds me close and tight as he runs his fingers through my hair. In typical DJ fashion, he lets me talk and take things at my own pace, knowing I'll tell him everything he wants to know as long as he gives me the time to do it.

Eventually, I take a deep breath. "It wasn't really that he didn't like the way I tasted," I mumble into his chest. "It's more that I gave and never got. Though, that's probably selfish. But mostly he always said I smelled. Even after I just got out of the shower, he would say that to me. And then he'd want sex. Which was three minutes of him moving over me, and me not being able to feel anything because he was so small. Like... not even the length of my hand. He wasn't even as long as the width of it. That kind of small." I hold up my hand for him to see. Though, I know he knows how small my hand is. He's held it before. He's kissed it before.

He kisses the top of my head and gently takes my hand. He links our fingers and rests our hands against his stomach. His hand engulfs mine. I love that. I've always loved how big he is compared to me.

"I know you said that because of his health issues he'd never be more developed mentally than a teenager, baby, but even teenagers know better than that. If you tell him that the way he talks hurts you, then he should understand that and correct the problem. And if he loved you at all, he would have."

"I know..."

"It just seems to me like you made excuse after excuse for him and tried to make it work, but he wouldn't change. Which means a few things. He didn't love you enough to change. And probably that he flat out wasn't capable of doing it. Which means his mental capacity was far worse than what you had been led to believe. That's not your fault. There isn't a damn thing you can do about it. Except exactly what you did, and that was to walk. No one deserves that kind of treatment."

"I know that now. But then... I guess I just didn't really think I could do better. I didn't want to be alone. I didn't want my family to be disappointed in me. So, I dealt with it. I didn't really need him for the sex part. I have toys. I settled for them. It's not like I enjoyed it with him. I mean, honestly, who would enjoy sex with someone who tells you that you're fat and that you smell? And, like I said, I couldn't feel him anyway. I always felt like such a terrible person, though. Like, I can't get off with my husband. I don't enjoy sex with him. I'd rather watch Pornhub and use a toy." I shake my head and sniffle.

He kisses the top of my head again. "I can tell you that you don't smell. I've seen how clean you are. Meaning, I know that you quite often clean yourself up and change your panties during the day if you feel like you need to. I've been around here long enough to see your laundry basket and hear the water running. It doesn't take a genius."

"I really am a clean person," I whisper. "I didn't take a shower every day, or a bath every day, because doing that strips the moisture from your skin. And if you don't really sweat a lot and stay clean anyway… And I only wash my hair once a week. Maybe twice depending if I sweat and it gets greasy. But that doesn't mean I didn't clean up. I stay clean."

I hear the deep rumble of a chuckle in my chest. "Rih, really. You don't need to explain your hygiene habits to me. I've seen them. I'm with you almost every day and night. You smell like coconut with a hint of something else that I can't quite figure out. And I can tell you with all honesty that when I go down on you, and I will whenever you're ready for it, that I'll enjoy every fucking second. There's no doubt in my mind that you taste as good as you smell."

I blush a deep shade of red at his words. But the promise in them makes me skip into a shade of dark purple. I'm positive that if he looked at my heated cheeks, he'd think I'm a chameleon.

"What if… I'm ready?" I ask barely above a whisper. I'm not even sure he heard me because he's silent for so long. I take a chance and look up at him. The sharp green of his eyes looks even more piercing. I inhale sharply.

He leans down and kisses me slowly. Deeply. His tongue crashes into mine again and again. I grip his shirt to keep myself from being pushed off the edge of whatever ledge I'm suddenly standing on. The passion behind the kiss takes my breath away. I whimper as he holds me in a vice-like grip against his chest.

He tugs my hair gently and kisses down my jaw to my throat. He licks it and kisses to the side of my neck as I moan softly. Every part of me ignites for him. Suddenly, I'm thinking of all the things I want him to do to me. All of the ways I want to come undone for him. Not a single thought is innocent or pure. They are all sinful and delectable.

I arch into him with a gasp when he grips my ass. He pulls me into him. It's hard to miss the outline of his large incredibly hard dick against my thigh. It does nothing to curb any of the thoughts he's put into my head.

He pulls back slowly. "Are you sure?"

I look deeply into his eyes and nod. "Yes."

He smiles and gently pushes me on my back. "Do you trust me?"

I nod again. "Implicitly."

"Good girl." He kisses me softly and gets up, making me instantly miss his rock solid everything against me. I watch him and almost start whining as I press my thighs together.

He digs in his duffle bag and pulls out a pair of handcuffs. My eyes widen as I tilt my head curiously. He stalks slowly to the bed. A sexy smile matches his cocky demeanor.

I lick my lips as he kneels on the bed next to me. "What are you planning?"

He smiles wickedly. "I thought you said you trusted me?"

"I do." I eye the handcuffs as he straddles me.

"Then trust me." He leans down and kisses me as he takes my hands.

He guides my arms over my head and holds my wrists. He puts a cuff on one hand and pulls it up, wrapping it around my bed frame. I watch his every movement as he slowly pulls away. He cuffs my other wrist and locks the handcuffs.

He leans down and kisses me again. I close my eyes and melt into his lips. His hands run ever so leisurely and tenderly down my arms. He moves slowly down my sides until he gets to the hem of my shirt. He pulls it just as slowly up my body. Just as I open my eyes, he moves my shirt over them.

I lick my lips and close my eyes again, giving into the feel of his fingertips on my skin. His lips and breath against my neck as he kisses down my collarbone to the mounds of my tits.

I moan when his tongue flicks my nipple. "Oh…" All at once I realize that I'm not wearing a bra. My triple D breasts are completely exposed to him. Fully out there for him to do with as he pleases.

For the first time in my life, I want it. I want all of it. I want to experience every single sensation I possibly can. All of the feelings I write about that I've never felt myself. That I've never cared to share with anyone.

His tongue lavishes my nipples in turn while he twists and tugs and rubs the one his mouth isn't attacking. I throw my head back and arch into him, moaning and panting for more, unable to use words.

I pull against the cuffs and arch when he growls against my nipples and blows air on them. "Oh… God."

My entire body tingles in anticipation as I give completely into just feeling. Feeling everything. Him. His lips. Breath. Fingers. Tongue. Hands. I arch, not able to get close enough. I tug harder against the cuffs and moan. My stomach clenches as I pant for him.

He pulls slowly away, keeping his hands against me. He trails them down my sides to the waistband of my shorts as he slides his tongue down and leaves kisses along my stomach. I whimper when I feel him sit back on his knees. But his hands don't leave my hips.

"Doing okay?" he asks huskily as he tucks his fingertips underneath my waistband.

"Mmhmm…" I bite my lip.

"Good girl." He tugs my shorts and panties down. Hard.

My hips jerk off the bed, and I slide down a little. My wrists pull hard against the cuffs. "Oh! DJ!"

He pulls them down just to my thighs. I try to maneuver and get them completely off, but he holds them where they are with one hand and turns me slightly. He slaps my ass. I inhale sharply.

"Patience. Feel. Nothing else."

I bite my lip again and nod. "Okay."

I feel him settle against my thigh. He leans down and kisses me pushing my legs apart as far as they will go being binded with my shorts and panties. His fingertips lightly graze my inner thigh as he makes his way up to where I'm aching for him.

When his tongue dives into my mouth, his finger dips into my pussy. His kiss muffles the scream that sneaks its way up. My hips vault off the bed.

I feel him smile into the kiss. "My girl likes that."

He thrusts hard and deep. Slow. I grind into his finger, meeting his thrusts. Tears sting my eyes as sensations I haven't even been able to give myself course through me. All of me. He takes me higher and higher until I'm so far above the ground, I'm terrified there's nowhere to land when I crash.

Just when I think it can't feel any better, DJ finds my clit and starts expertly touching it. Rubbing. Flicking. I forget how to breathe as my body completely takes on a mind of its own. My brain shuts down. All I can feel is him. He's my life.

I barely register when his lips kiss down my body once more. Or when he pushes my shorts down to my ankles allowing my legs to fall apart for him. Only him.

His thumb continues teasing my clit as I writhe. He replaces the finger inside me with his tongue. I scream and launch up to meet his tongue. Tears stream down my face. I can taste the salt on my tongue from the ones my shirt failed to catch.

"DJ! Ah!"

He cockily smirks against my pussy as his tongue darts in and out of me at a pace that makes me dizzy. "My girl really likes that." He licks up to my clit then back down.

"DJ. Oh my… God…" I pull against the cuffs harder and harder as he ravishes me.

"I was right. You taste as sweet as you smell."

My world tilts upside down and spins out of control. My pussy tightens as hard as my stomach. He continues his masterful domination of my clit as I clench hard around his tongue. I try to close my legs as my clit starts throbbing and pulsing and tingling far more intensely than I've ever managed to make it do on my own. He holds my legs open.

"DJ! I… I'm gonna…"

He smiles against my pussy and sucks as he flicks my clit. "Come, baby. Come for me. Give me all that sweetness."

I arch into him trembling. I throw my head back and shiver as my entire body jerks. My pussy pulses and tightens around his tongue. I come harder than I ever imagined possible. I wouldn't be able to stop it if I tried.

I feel it throughout my entire body. Like it's being ripped from so deep within me, it explodes and will never be able to be rebuilt. Captain DJ Rens has both destroyed me and brought me to life all at the same time.

When it's over, and I sense the bed underneath me once more, I feel my cheeks are tear-soaked. DJ uncuffs me and pulls the shirt off my eyes and over my arms. I blink against the light as he slowly comes back into focus. He's straddling me.

He leans down and kisses me so softly, the tears start again. Being it's DJ, I don't have to explain what I need or how I feel. He instinctively moves to my side and takes me in his strong, protective arms. He holds me close and tight while I cry like a fool.

The wave of emotions coursing through me is beyond overwhelming. I've never come for anyone other than myself before. And even then, I wasn't sure that I did. I've never felt the tidal wave of sensation flow through me like this. I've never felt even a fraction of what I feel right now. I've never felt this sense of peace. I feel myself melt into his strong embrace as I realize I've finally found what I have been blindly searching for all these years.

This sense of belonging.

Of being wanted. Truly wanted.

This sense of…

Home.

Chapter Eight

★ DJ ★

Waking up next to a naked Mariah the next morning has become my new favorite way to wake up. I was far too tired last night to remove anything more than my shirt, so I'm still wearing jeans. Mariah is wrapped around me.

I smile into her hair and lightly brush my lips across her forehead. After I made her come last night, she cried herself to sleep. She didn't have to tell me that it was because no one had ever taken the time to do it. But I knew it was more than that. Something far deeper.

No one had ever cared enough about Mariah or her happiness to ever do anything just for her. It wasn't just the sex for her. It was that I'm the first person who cares about her enough to not only tell her, but also show her that she's worth it.

She's worth the time it takes to please *her*. She's worth the effort it takes to make *her* happy and take care of *her* needs. To put *her* above me. No one has ever done that for her before. And for the life of me, I don't understand why. Mariah is by far the most selfless person I've ever met. Why anyone wouldn't want to treat her like the most precious of diamonds is something I can't wrap my head around.

I've seen Mariah give more of herself to strangers over the past couple of months than I've ever seen anyone give to anyone. She never asks for anything in return. What I gave her last night was only a small way of showing her that she deserves more than what she's gotten. She deserves to be treated better. She deserves everything.

I gently and slowly start to get up, but her fingertips dig into my side. "Stay...," she says sleepily.

I smile. "Honey, I need to take a shower and get ready for work."

She groans. "GPD can't have you today. Stay..."

I laugh and shift slightly. I take her face in my hands and lift her chin so she's looking at me. "Last day. Then I'm all yours for a few days." I lean down and kiss her softly. "Besides, you have a busy day ahead of you. That book ain't going to write itself."

She smiles and giggles. "When it's going well, it can write itself."

I smile and kiss her again as I grip her ass. I pull her close as she melts into me. "I'd like to see a book write itself. You sitting there drinking some iced tea. Your book just throwing words up on the screen for you." I give her a teasing smile.

She pushes against my chest and laughs. "Go to work!"

I smile wider and grip her wrists and pull her back to me. "I will. But first..." I let go of her wrists after I kiss them. I slide my hand down her body making sure to squeeze her tits and flick her nipples on my way to her sweet center.

Her eyes widen and she moans when I slide my middle finger deep within her. I kiss her and thrust slow and deep and hard. She submits completely to me. She grips my arm and closes her eyes as her head falls back.

"Oh..."

I feel her pussy pulsing around my finger. I kiss her throat. "I think making you come is one of my new favorite hobbies."

She arches into me and grips my hair as I kiss her neck. "DJ..."

She almost instantly tightens when I start teasing her clit with my thumb. I thrust faster. Her fingers dig into my arm. She clenches around my finger and breathes out a breathy moan. I thrust harder and faster, rubbing her clit at the same pace I'm thrusting. When she starts trembling and whimpering for me, I kiss her long and deeply.

"Come, my girl."

"Oh my God." She obeys and comes hard, soaking my finger. I keep thrusting, slowing my pace. She kisses me between moans and jerks as her body spasms. "DJ. Oh God."

"You're so tight, honey."

She opens her eyes slowly and looks at me with the sweetest, most content look I've ever seen on any woman I've ever been with. I kiss her forehead and slow my thrusts more and more as she comes down.

When she's relaxed, I pull gently out of her and suck her taste off my finger as I get up. "Told ya you were sweet." I throw a wink over my shoulder as she blushes that pretty shade of pink and hides in her pillows. I lean down and slap her ass as I head for the shower.

"Hey!" She looks at me and laughs as I walk to the bathroom.

After I'm through with my shower, I head out to her bedroom. My mouth instantly waters at the smell of bacon. I groan as I quickly get dressed. I strap my gun belt to my shoulder. One of the good things about being a Captain is I don't always have to wear a uniform. I check my gun and put it in its holster, then walk out of the bedroom.

Mariah is swaying to no music as she finishes plating bacon, eggs, hashbrowns and toast. She licks something off her finger and tilts her head, like she's trying to figure out if she forgot something.

She catches my eye and smiles. "I was hoping I'd get it done before you had to leave."

I look at my watch. "I have time, honey." I walk to her and sit down at the bar on one of the barstools. She slides my plate to me as she walks around and sits next to me. "Tomatoes, onions, mushrooms, cheese, and peppers on the hashbrowns?" I smile down at her.

"I remembered."

"I love my hash browns like this. I haven't had a lot of time to make them like this, so this is a treat." I dig in, savoring every bite. She watches me as she quietly eats with a soft smile. When we're done, she starts to get up to clean up. I get up and kiss her cheek as I take her plate. "I got it."

"Oh... It's okay. I can do it. You need to start getting ready to head out."

"Mariah." I turn towards her. "I got it, honey. This is a relationship. Give and take. You cooked. Least I can do is clean up." It's nothing I haven't told her several times over the course of our relationship. I'll keep telling her for as long as it takes for her to believe me.

She smiles softly and bites her lip. "I'm just… not used to you. It's never been like this for me. I cooked. I cleaned. Near the end, I'll be honest. I sort of gave up. I cooked when I had to and cleaned when I didn't have a choice, but mostly, I just did everything."

"You don't need to do that anymore. I'm here for you. We're a team."

"Everything is so different for me with you." She stands at my side and starts drying dishes. "I'm just not used to anything. I'm not used to the person I'm with wanting to cuddle. I'm not used to the touch not being repulsive to me. Like…, you touch me, or lean against me, or even take my hand and kiss it. When he did that, I cringed. And it was only when he wanted to. If I touched him? It was 'I'm sick' or 'don't, it's too hot.' But when I didn't want to be touched I was a horrible person. I'm just…" She looks up at me. "I'm just not used to any of this."

I finish the last dish and hand it to her to dry. "Baby, I can't believe the amount of mental abuse you endured. And not just mental. Emotional. I mean, I know you've been telling me little things here and there, but I know there's so much more. I can tell because when I do things like call you beautiful, you almost cry." I gesture to the dishes. "Just doing this almost brought you to tears. And I've done this before."

She looks down and crosses her arms over her chest as she leans against the counter. "It's really just been a constant thing. My whole life. I was always made to feel like I'm fat. Even when I was a cheerleader. I was never the smallest of people. But still. I was never made to feel pretty. I've always been made to believe that it's my job to clean and cook. My dad never did much. My stepmom didn't either. If I wanted a clean house, I did it myself. I never had help."

"So what you're telling me is you came from a life where you were made to feel like nothing more than a maid and unpretty. And you went into a life where you were made to feel like a maid and unpretty. Unworthy of being loved the way you should be." I cock my hip against the counter and run my fingers through her hair. "Do you see the cycle?"

She refuses to meet my eyes. "I see it. And I'm trying to break it," she says quietly. "Really. I am. I'm really trying to force my mind to believe everything you tell me. And what really doesn't make sense is that

I do believe it. I know you're not lying to me. But as soon as the words start to sink in, my mind just starts thinking of everything else that's gone on. The words of others. Their actions. All of it just plays against me."

"Rih, honey, that's you overthinking everything. And trust me. You aren't the only person in the world who deals with it. It's your anxiety. When I don't text you back right away, you start wondering why. Your mind races from he's busy, which is the truth, to he just don't want to talk to me, which is so far from the truth, it's comical. And then you skip right into thinking that you did something wrong and upset me. You're so used to being blamed for the actions of others, you put blame on yourself when it doesn't belong there." I run my thumb over her lower lip and lean down to kiss her. "I know me just sitting here saying that you have to take things for what they are and quit imagining the worst doesn't help you."

She shakes her head. "It really doesn't."

"But... I do know that actions speak louder than words. Which is why I have no issues with telling you how beautiful you are all the time. Or explaining to you that I've been in meetings or on calls and am not mad at you. I don't mind showing you everyday how I feel about you. Do you know why? "

"No..."

I kiss her again and again until she's giggling. I smile. "Because you're worth so much more than you think you are. You're worth the time. Effort. You're worth it all."

"Thank you. For getting me out of my head." She stands on her tiptoes to kiss me, but I stand taller, just out of her reach. She laughs. "Such an ass." She swats my chest.

I give in and kiss her. "Good girl. I gotta go." I catch her chin and make her look at me as I smile. "I'm falling in love with you. You know that?"

Her eyes light up. "Really?"

"Really."

She smiles so brightly she could rival the sun. I love when she does that. "I'm falling in love with you, too."

I grin just as magnificently at her declaration. I kiss her again and again before I force myself to pull away and head for the door. I grab my duffle bag with all of my gear for work in it and sling it over my shoulder. I open the door and watch as a white piece of paper falls to the ground.

"Oh no…"

I glance at my girl before checking the hall. Seeing no one, I bend to pick up the note. I glare at it as I close the door and put my duffle bag back down. Mariah looks at me completely terrified as I open the note. I don't read it out loud.

Mariah,

I tried hard to get your attention. But you still don't notice me. I've sent you so many DM's over the past few weeks. I've sent so many love notes. Presents. And still. You don't notice me. That bear I sent you. I saw it ripped apart in the garbage bin. I told you how hurt I was about that. But I understood. I thought maybe it was too fast.

I sent you flowers. I sent you poems. But you ignored me. You ignored me, Mariah. You didn't notice me. You didn't acknowledge me.

Instead, you were with that asshole. That stupid fucking cop. He touched you. You let him put his hands all over you. He had his tongue inside you! Don't you understand that you're mine? You've always been mine! Ever since I first saw you at the Depot!

But you let HIM HAVE YOU!

Now, you have to learn your lesson. You have to learn that you belong to me. You won't get away with letting him have what I want. What's mine, Mariah. You won't get away with letting him taste you.

I'm tired of watching you with him. I'm tired of seeing you share breakfast and dinner. I'm the one you're supposed to share things with! I don't like watching you in the bath without me! I don't like you cuddling on the couch with him watching movies. I'm supposed to be the one holding you! ME!

Time for you to come home where you belong, Mariah. The house is set up. We have all we need to finally start our happily ever after. All that's missing is you. But not for long.

I'm not playing anymore. I'm done waiting. I'm coming for you.

Yours Only,
X

I put the note in my pocket and take Mariah's hand. I lock the door and drag her to the bedroom. I pull out a gym bag and a duffel bag and start throwing things into it.

"DJ?" she asks quietly.

I look up, realizing I'm scaring the hell out of her. I stop and walk to her. I take her face in my hands and look her deep in her ice blue eyes. "We need to leave. You can't stay here. You need to trust me right now. I'll explain. But not here. Not now."

She searches my eyes as she shakily grips my wrists. "I trust you."

I kiss her before letting her go. She jumps into action and begins grabbing her necessities. Within minutes, we're walking out the door, her hand tightly in mine. I fight the urge to grab my gun as I lead her to my car, but I keep my eyes open and scan everything around us.

My eyes fall on the orange Dodge Charger with tinted windows and racer stripes at the edge of the lot positioned with a perfect view of the door to Mariah's building. There's no other cars around it. It's not in a parking place. I've always considered myself observant. No fucking way I wouldn't have noticed that car before.

No plates on the front draws my eye to it for more reasons than just flashiness. My experience tells me that a car without a front plate is either asking for trouble or is trouble. There is no in between.

I put Mariah's things in the backseat of my car, keeping her right next to me as I glare at the car. I guide her towards the driver's seat. "Crawl across. Buckle in."

Her gaze follows mine, but she does as she's told. "Okay." She quickly ducks inside and crawls across the seat.

She buckles into the passenger seat. On the other side of her is an SUV. She's protected from being seen or anything else by that car. I silently thank whoever parked there last night after I got here.

I take out my phone and call Matt, keeping my eyes on the Charger. I stand in the door of my car and rest my arms on the roof. I want whoever that is to know I'm watching. Even though I can't see in the windshield, I want to make sure whoever it is knows they've caught my attention.

"Hey, DJ. Where the hell are you? Huge case came in -"

"I don't care. Listen. Mariah's stalker has escalated and -"

Mariah screams. "DJ! Look out!"

I feel the hit before I have a chance to react in any way whatsoever. I fall to my knees next to a metal baseball bat. The last thing I see before I lose consciousness is Mariah screaming as she lunges for me. She's violently yanked back by her seatbelt as my attacker appears at her door.

"Danny…" I growl out, instantly recognizing the conceited kid who has rubbed me the wrong way since I met him.

He gives me a vile smile, yanking Mariah out of my car. Her screams echo in my ears as my world goes dark.

Chapter Nine

☆ Mariah ☆

"DJ!" I yell as I lunge for him. I reach down to unbuckle my seatbelt as I scramble towards him. I fumble as I scream for him. "DJ!"

I don't know who knocked him out. I couldn't see that. But I know he was talking to Matt. Matt had to hear. He'll send help. I know he will. I just have to get to DJ. I have to help him.

I scream again as soon as my seatbelt snaps against my chest. I fly back into my seat. I look up to see Danny's face giving me a sadistic grin. He viciously grabs my arm and reaches over to me to unsnap my seatbelt.

I try scrambling for DJ again as he growls Danny's name. He falls to the ground. Danny pulls me back against him, but I fight. I kick and scream. I grip the steering wheel and pull myself towards DJ and out of Danny's grasp.

"Mariah! Don't make me hurt you!"

"DJ!" I turn enough so I can slap and claw at Danny. Anything to get away from him.

"Stop fighting me!" He slaps me. Hard. I blink, dazed, but keep kicking at him.

"Get away from me! Help! Help us!" I slap him back as hard as I can manage as I flail against him.

"Bitch!"

Focus. I have to focus. I have to get away from him somehow. I have to gain the attention of someone. Anyone. Someone has to hear me. Someone has to be around. At least close enough to see me.

Matt. He has to still be on the phone. He has to hear me. "Matt! Matt, it's Danny!" I yell it as loudly as I can. I don't know if DJ has his phone. I don't know if it went flying somewhere. "Matt! Help! It's, Danny! It's -"

"Stop! Stop it!" Danny screams as he yanks me out of the car and hits me. The blow knocks me to the ground.

I immediately start crying as I scream. "Matt! Help! It's Danny!" I spot DJ's phone near the rear tire.

"Stop screaming!" Danny yells. He kicks me in the stomach.

I reach for the phone and scramble to get away. Danny catches me, but I have time to stuff the phone in my bra. I pray he didn't see as I fight him. Anything to get away.

But I don't have any more time to scream or fight or run. Danny punches me hard in the side of the head. I gasp out Matt's name one more time, imploring any God listening to make sure he hears my plea as I black out.

☆☆☆

I groan as I come to. The pain in my head is excruciating. Like a million nails being shoved into my brain.

One by one.

Slowly.

Torturously slowly.

I can't move because when I do everything spins. I'm not convinced I'm on Earth. For all I know, I could be in some other galaxy beyond any known galaxies.

The thought of opening my eyes sends my heart into a race to see who can win. Will it be my stomach for throwing up? Or my heart for beating out of my chest and starting its own campaign to destroy me? One piercing puncture at a time.

Instead of allowing any part of my panicking body to dominate me, I stay totally still. I listen for sounds. I focus on smells. Feel. Taste. All of my senses. But not only to stave off a panic attack. That's only an added bonus.

No.

I know enough to know that what I'm doing is forcing survival mode. I need to fight to live. I need to be calm. Think rationally. I refuse to allow my anxiety to get in the way of that. And the only way for me to keep it at bay is to focus on anything else.

I take a deep breath and open my eyes.

Slowly.

I look around, realizing that I'm in a bedroom on a large, four post bed. I'm lying on my side, but I don't move. I need to focus. Make certain I'm alone in the room. I feel nothing restraining my arms or hands. There's nothing restraining my legs. Feet.

Wait.

I move my right foot ever so slightly.

Damn... No...

I choke down a sob when I feel metal on my ankle. I'm cuffed to one of the posts by my foot. I take another silent, deep breath and chance more slight movements, giving me more visual of the room. I lean ever so gently back and look over my shoulder.

There's no one in the bed. Thank God. I move more, but still slowly. I don't want to risk alerting anyone to anything. I scan the room. It's light enough to see if anyone is hiding in the corners. There's no one.

I breathe a quiet sigh of relief and turn very slowly back to my side. I know DJ. I know that he wouldn't make me leave in that much of a rush if something didn't scare him. I've had this stalker for a while. He's trusted that I'll be okay in my apartment with the doors locked when he's not there. I don't leave it without him or Lyric or Matt.

That means something in the recent letter set him off. Maybe a threat? The threat of this? I stay still as I think.

Think like DJ. I have to think like him. The threat would have definitely set him into motion on getting me out. But... I chew the inside of my cheek. There's more. I feel it. I know DJ. He would never jump into action without telling me what's happening. He'd be flying around my room throwing clothes in duffel bags, but he'd talk to me. He'd tell me why as he's doing it.

DJ didn't do that. His eyes darted all over the place. He said he'd tell me later. Trust him. It was an action so far out of everything I know about him.

I stare at the wall. I don't know how long I've been out, but I'm truly hoping that it wasn't more than a few hours. I don't want that much time gone. Time is all I have right now. And I can feel it slipping from my grasp.

I mentally shake my head. I have to think. DJ acted so quickly. Like we were being watched.

I suck in a sharp breath and close my eyes.

Watched.

Cameras. In my apartment.

I shiver as the realization hits me. That means he was in my house when I wasn't. Or maybe he was in there while I was there. Tears sting my eyes as I whimper.

But why? Why wouldn't he have made a move before this? If he could get to me any other time, why today? If he was watching me, he knew when I was alone. Why would he not take me then?

No.

No. I can't let my mind wander. I have to concentrate on getting out of here. Nothing else. I can't think of anything but trying to figure out where I am.

I sniffle thinking of DJ. I don't know if he's okay. I don't know what Danny did to him after he knocked me out. What if he killed him?

I mentally shake my head again.

No. I can't think like that. DJ is okay.

I focus on my surroundings. Any sounds. Smells. Anything that can help me.

After a few minutes, I hear water. Like a speed boat or jet ski moving through it. Voices. Happy voices. Laughter.

It smells fresh. Like cedar and rain. Crystal clear air.

A resort?

All at once, I remember DJ's phone. I slowly move my hand from my stomach to my chest. I reach into my bra and feel it.

"Thank God," I whisper. "Please, please still work."

I take it slowly out of my bra looking and listening for any movement. I leave it down my shirt and push the side button. Matt's number is still connected. Somehow. I'll never be more grateful to see his name.

I whimper when I see that the battery is getting dangerously low. I put it on speaker anyway, taking a chance.

"Matt?" I whisper. "Please, please still be there."

"Mariah?" His voice is low and barely above a whisper. I silently thank him for picking up on my cue to be quiet.

"Thank God. Oh my God, thank God." I keep my sobs at bay, but let the tears silently fall.

"Mariah, we're tracking DJ's phone, but we lost the signal. We think he has a scrambler. You just went dark. At first, I thought the phone died, but we could still hear everything. I've been muted on my end so he can't hear me talk, but we've been listening."

"The battery. It's almost dead." I quietly sniffle.

"Fuck, I was afraid of that. Listen to me. I need you to listen to your surroundings. I need you to listen for anything that might give me a clue to where you are. I lost you on the outskirts of Gainesville. It looks like he was heading South."

"I hear water. Like… speed boats on the water. I hear jet skiing. And there's kids and people laughing."

"Can you tell if you're on one or two floors?"

"It looks like one. It doesn't look like I'm high, but I'm too scared to move too much. One of my feet are cuffed to the bed. And I don't know if he's watching me."

"Okay. How much battery is left?"

I look and nearly start sobbing. "It's flashing," I whisper with a small squeak.

"Ssh… It's okay. I need you to look around. You have to see if there are any notepads or pens with a name. Anything, Mariah. Give me something."

"Tell me how DJ is. Distract me."

"DJ was knocked out. He's okay, but he hasn't come to yet."

I let out a small gasp and sniffle as I chance moving to my elbow enough to see the nightstand. "I see a pen…"

"Good. Look at it. Tell me what it says."

I shakily reach for it, not wanting to alert Danny in any way that I'm awake. But the bed creaks under my weight. I bite my lip to keep from letting any sound out of my mouth. I quickly take the pen.

"Lochloosa." My eyes snap to the door when I hear footsteps. "He's coming!" I whisper as softly as I can over my panic.

"Pretend like you're sleeping. Hide the phone and pen. We're coming for you. You aren't far away. Just hang in there, M-"

The phone dies as I shove it down with the pen into my bra. I snap my eyes closed and burrow into the pillow beneath my head hugging myself as the door opens.

I'm convinced my heart can be heard miles away, but I force my breathing to remain even and steady. I can't let anyone know that I'm awake. I can't let Danny know that I know where we are. Or that Matt is coming.

I feel him sit next to me. I flinch internally when he pushes my hair out of my eyes. But I don't move. I don't open my eyes. I don't whimper. I don't cry. I want to fight him, but I keep from moving at all. I do nothing more than breathe.

Just breathe.

"You're so beautiful, Mariah. You'll understand how good we can be together. Just as soon as our house is ready. I didn't expect there to be a problem with the plumbing. But don't worry. It's getting fixed."

I'll never be with you. Never. I can feel myself start to shiver. I try to stop it, but nothing I do helps. My stomach clenches. My skin feels like it's crawling.

"Are you cold? I should have thought of that." He gets up. I hug myself tighter, willing my body to obey my commands.

Suddenly, I can hear DJ's voice in my head. I can feel his love and warmth envelope me. *You have to calm down, Mariah. The only way we can beat him is to stay calm.*

Just like that, I'm calm. His scent surrounds me. His strength fills me. It's been two incredible months. The best of my life. I won't let Danny ruin it. I won't let him win. I won't let him beat me at whatever sick game he's begun with me.

He sits down next to me and puts a blanket over me. "I'm sorry it had to be like this. If only you'd listened to me before. If only you wouldn't have ignored me. I hate being ignored, Mariah. You shouldn't have ignored me." He tucks the blanket around me. "You shouldn't have let that idiot cop have you. I can protect you just like he can. I tried to show you. But you let him whisk you away."

Keep him talking, Rih, DJ's voice whispers. I move ever so slightly making sure I lean gently into his hand. Like it's comforting.

As I hoped, Danny runs his fingers through my hair and keeps talking. "Ever since I first saw you, I knew you were meant for me. I made sure that if you were at an event, I was there, too. Even if the security firm I worked for wasn't the firm hired for the event security. I wanted to make sure you were safe. One of your events last month, someone tried to cut in line. He was really aggressive. He was talking about how he needed to see you before he ran out of time, and it was talking too long. He said that he was going to tell you to hurry. You have too many people there." He pauses. I can feel his eyes on me. His grip tightens just slightly on my hair.

Where are you going with this, Danny? I ask myself the question, but I'm positive I don't want to know the answer.

He continues running his fingers through my hair. "I really didn't have a choice. I told him that I worked your security. I showed him my security badge. I told him I could take him to you. He said he was your biggest fan, but that he had to go soon. He had to see you. He wanted his book autographed. I took him to the bathroom. He was confused. I told him that I won't let anyone hurt you. I strangled him."

The words send chills to the core of my stomach. He says the words so naturally. Like killing someone is a normal, everyday occurrence.

Calm, Mariah. We're coming for you. DJ's voice in the back of my mind keeps me from letting the scream bubbling up escape. I stay still. I keep my eyes closed.

"I got rid of him. I took him to the woods behind the venue."

Sick son of a bitch. I keep my hand from clenching.

"A couple of weeks ago, this woman came onto me at an event we were running security for. I told her I had someone. She didn't care. She was drunk. I led her outside to my car and used my necktie to take the life from her. My body is yours, Mariah. No one else's. I kissed her. But don't be upset. It didn't mean anything. I had to convince her to go with me. I'll make up for it." The fingers he was running through my hair make their

86

way down my back. He stops on my ass and squeezes. "Just like you'll make up for your indiscretions."

He gets up as tears sting my eyes. *I'll make you pay for touching me, you fucker.*

"Get some sleep, my Mariah. In the morning, we have a big day. Lots to talk about. Like which room we're going to sleep in. Which you'd like for your office. When we're getting married. If we want kids. I have to go to work. I'll be back soon."

I can't help but wonder how many more people he killed. When I hear the door close and hear his footsteps fade, I let out a long breath. I wait, listening for the door to close before I sit up and look at my surroundings more.

The cuff around my foot is actually more than just a cuff. I hadn't noticed since I hadn't moved, but there's a long chain attached to it. I have a lot more freedom to move than I thought.

The room is a little larger than my first impression. There's what looks to be a small private patio. Next to the bathroom looks to be luggage. Not mine.

"I wonder…" I listen for a few more minutes, making sure he's gone and no one else is around. As quietly as I can, I get up off the bed. I close my eyes against the dizziness and sit on the edge of the bed for a few moments. I touch my head gingerly and feel dried blood. "Fuck…"

I slowly get up and walk to the luggage. I kneel next to it and start opening the bags. I dig in all of them, moving clothing aside looking for anything that might be able to help me. Keys to the cuffs. A phone. A charger. Anything.

I find a manilla envelope at the bottom of one of them. Several manilla envelopes. I glance towards the door as I start opening them.

"Oh… my God…" I pull out photographs of myself at different events I've been at over the past few weeks. There's images of DJ with me. Us kissing. There's photos of me with Matt. And others with me and Lyric. There's a bunch of papers with times and descriptions. I blink back tears when I realize that they are journal entries.

He knows when I go to the bathroom. When I cook breakfast. He knows when I start writing and take breaks. He knows when I bathe. His descriptions are detailed. Like… Like he's watching my every move.

"Cameras. You really did have cameras." The tears break free. I sob as I continue looking through files.

He has a file for the guy he said he killed. Pictures of him. Dead. I cry harder and pick up the next envelope. It's of the woman he said he killed from the event he was at. So many horrific images. My heart breaks over and over again the more I look.

They aren't the only two he's killed. I find three more envelopes with other victims. The descriptions are that they are fans who he decided were causing issues at my events. Events he wasn't even security for.

There is a folder for Matt, DJ, and Lyric. All with personal photos of them. At work. On calls. At home. With me. There's one with a huge 'X' and a hole through Matt's face where he's hugging me. The description he wrote on the back simply says, 'he can't have what's mine.'

I wipe my eyes as I continue looking. He has detailed schedules for all three of them along with a date that he plans to end them. I assume he means kill.

"Oh God." My eyes widen when I see the date next to DJ, Matt, and Lyric as today. Next to DJ's name he says completed. My mouth drops. "He thought he killed him!"

I force myself to look more through the luggage. I have to find a charger. Or phone. Anything. I cry even more frustrated when I don't find one. I look around the room again. There has to be a phone. But the nightstand where it should be is empty.

I take a deep breath. "You have to have a charger." I dump everything out of the bags and look through all of the pockets. Finally, in the last bag, I find a charger. "Yes!"

I scramble, looking for an outlet. I find one and quickly plug in the phone. I jump up excitedly when it works for DJ's phone.

After a few moments, it's charged enough to allow me to make a phone call. I quickly dial Matt. He said he was coming for me.

I only pray that he makes it in time.

Chapter Ten

★ DJ ★

"Mariah? You okay?" Matt asks. My eyes snap open. I sit up with a groan ignoring the stabbing pain in the back of my head. I feel like I'm upside down, but I don't give a shit.

"Mariah?" I grab Matt's arm as Lyric tries to get me to lay back down. I love her to death, but I shoot her a withering glare that has her backing down and away instantly, flinching.

Matt holds up a hand. "What?" He listens for a second. "Okay. Okay. I have a team coming here. We're all going together. DJ is awake. He's okay." He hands me the phone as he gets up and gathers his gun and SWAT gear.

"Mariah?"

"DJ?"

My heart both races and calms at her voice. "Fuck. What happened? Are you okay?"

"He has me at a resort in Hawthorne. I think. Lochloosa? He has a chain cuff around my ankle." She sniffles. "I can't leave the room. But I found things. I think he's going after Matt and Lyric because he feels like they are a threat to his happiness with me. He has files, DJ."

"Did you tell Matt?"

"I just told him that I found a lot of stuff, and I found a charger. And that I'm okay. And that he said he was leaving for work. I heard him go. I had your phone. I hid it. He didn't see me hide it. I was fighting and screaming. He knocked me out."

"I'm going to kill him." I run my hand down my face and shake my head slightly. "Are you okay?"

"I just came to a little while ago. He came in here before he left. He admitted to killing a couple of people. I found files of his victims. There's so much stuff, DJ. He thinks he killed you. He's after Matt and Lyric. I can't make sense of it all. I've been trying to just focus on surviving and getting out of here. But I keep slipping back into mini panic attacks. Then I hear your voice in my head guiding me. I'm so up and down. My mind is racing with everything I found."

I can tell she's close to going into a full blown panic attack by how quickly she's talking. Like she's trying to keep up with her own thoughts. Which are going two hundred miles an hour.

"Focus, baby." I look over my shoulder as Lyric hovers nearby watching me with concern. "We have a team showing up right now. We're all leaving in a couple of minutes. Please, please just stay calm and focused."

"Distract me. Tell me what happened to you. If you're okay."

I listen to Matt directing the team as they all strap equipment and bulletproof vests on. I walk over to them and start strapping on my own equipment. I'm grateful as fuck that Matt knows me well enough to have thought to grab my stuff from my car when he got to me in the parking lot of Mariah's building.

"I was hit in the back of the neck with something. I'm a little sore. It knocked me out. Matt must have gotten there because I just came to. I'm at his house on the couch. I just glared at Lyric. Shouldn't have." I hold out my arm for Lyric. She bites her lip and looks at me but doesn't move.

"Lyric hates when she thinks people are upset with her."

"I know, baby." My eyes soften as I watch Lyric. She hesitantly takes a few steps forward before she pauses and searches my eyes. I give her a small, reassuring smile. She finally scurries to me and burrows into me. I hug her as her fingers grip my shirt tightly. "I'm okay. I don't really know what happened. I saw Danny before I lost consciousness."

"I heard you say his name," she whispers. "Is Lyric okay? She must be scared."

"She's okay. Here. Want to talk to her? I need to get my gear on. So does she because she ain't staying here if there's a chance she's a target."

"Yes. I want to talk to her."

I put the phone to Lyric's ear as I kiss the top of her head. I really don't want to give up talking to her, but I have to get ready to go. Getting to Mariah is my priority.

"You're absolutely not going in, DJ," Matt says to me as he straps a gun to his leg.

"Not upon entry. But when you clear it, I'm going in for Mariah." I strap my vest on. "Thanks for grabbing my stuff from my car."

"I almost didn't, but I figured you had your backup guns in there. Why the fuck didn't he disarm you?"

"Because Mariah was screaming. I think he wanted to get out before she garnered too much attention."

"He knocked her out. So, I'm sure that didn't help. Probably why he didn't grab the bat he hit you with."

I reach up and touch the back of my head and neck. "I have no idea where he hit. I don't feel blood. My neck hurts like a fucker, though."

"I think he got you at the base of your skull. Lyric didn't see any cuts. You weren't bleeding. Vitals were normal, according to the paramedics. Doctor I talked to a little while ago thought you might have had a concussion. You were out maybe two hours. Mariah was smart enough to grab your phone. She must have hidden it because I heard her. I heard him talking to her. I could hear everything. The car taking off. Everything."

"She's very smart." I finish strapping my gear on. "Where are we with all of this? Where is she? She said she thinks Hawthorne."

"That's what the pen she found says. Lochloosa. We think he has a scrambler. We tried tracking the phone. But the last hit we got was from the outskirts of Gainesville. That would have been just about when I got to the apartment building. After that, there's nothing. But I knew he was driving. I could hear it. I heard when he stopped. It wasn't far. He was saying shit like he'll let her sleep. He'll check on her. She woke up not long ago. She must have remembered the phone. He came back in just as the phone died."

"Luckily she found a charger. And a fuck of a lot of shit to help us put him away for a long time."

He raises an eyebrow. "Like what?"

"Files. He apparently killed a couple people and kept records. He has records of the three of us. He thinks he killed me. You and Lyric are targets."

"She told me he left. She's alone. She said he has a few files. But then I gave her to you."

"Did you have anyone search the apartment?"

"No. My focus was you and her. You never told me what freaked you out."

I reach in my pocket and feel for the note. "Fuck. Yes. It's still here." I hand it to him.

He reads it. "Holy shit." He pulls out a phone from his pocket as he hands me back the note. "I've been using Lyric's phone since I've had Mariah on mine. I'll call tech. Tell them to get over there. But if he had cameras set up…"

I nod. "It means he had been in her apartment. And means it's possible he has a camera on her right now." I turn back to Lyric after I have my gear on. I signal for the phone. She smiles and says goodbye to Mariah as she hands it to me. She quickly throws her gear on.

"Mariah, honey, I don't want to alarm you, but I need to know. Cameras. Do you think he has a camera on you?"

She takes a sharp breath. "I was just telling Lyric I feel like I'm being watched. Is that why we left so fast?"

"That note said he'd been watching you. He knew that we had been together. He knew I had my tongue in you. He mentioned baths and other things."

"I found a whole journal. Like dates and everything. My whole schedule. When I bathed and ate. When I started working. He even says when you arrive and leave. He has Lyric's and Matt's schedule, but it's not as detailed."

"Matt and Lyric have a high-tech security system. I think he was able to pick your lock. He'd never be able to do that at mine or Matt's house."

"I don't see anything that looks like a camera. But I don't really know…"

"Look for stuffed animals. Things that just don't seem to belong."

She's quiet for a few moments, but I can hear her looking. "There's a pen on the desk in the bedroom. It has the name of his security company."

I follow Matt and Lyric out as we rush to the vehicles. I jump in next to Matt in his truck. He puts a red magnetic light up on his roof and takes off after squads and other vehicles. I don't know how he did it, but we have both County and State officers in our little posse. We speed towards Hawthorne.

"She found a pen with his security company written on it," I say to Matt.

He expertly steers through traffic keeping up with all of the other squads like a pro. "How was it facing?"

"Um…," Mariah begins, hearing him. "The cap was facing the bed." She's quiet a second. "Oh my God. DJ, it is a camera!"

I look at Matt horrified as I pick up the radio. "Are we on our own channel?"

"We're on our SWAT channel. All the squads with us are."

"All squads," I say into the mic. "She found a camera. We're running at Code Three."

"DJ! I think he's coming back!"

I watch as the squads in front of me step on it and all start driving faster. I glance at Matt. "This thing even do a hundred?"

He smirks and hits the gas. "I have a Hemi. You have to be kidding me." I watch as his speedometer kicks up past a hundred as he, once again, keeps up with the squads without any issues.

"Mariah, we're coming, baby. You have to fight for me." Tears sting my eyes. I feel helpless. The terrain flies by us, but I can't do anything to help my girl. I grip the phone harder listening with all I am.

"DJ!" She screams.

"How did you get a phone?" Danny screams. "Why are you doing this to me? To us?"

"Mariah! We're coming!" I shakily look at Matt. "He's there. He's fucking there."

93

"That camera. He could see her. We're not far. We're almost there. With the rate of speed, it won't be long. She has to fight, DJ."

Lyric cries in the backseat as I listen. There's scuffling. Screaming. I hear punches being thrown. Things like tables moving. My heart is no longer beating. I'm gripping Matt's dash so hard my knuckles are turning white. I don't know how the phone in my hand isn't broken.

"Ah!" Mariah screams again. "Get away from me! Get off me! Ah!"

"I trusted you! I trusted you not to snoop around! It's none of your business!" Danny screams back. Something else crashes as Mariah screams and cries.

"Fuck. Matt..." I look at him pleadingly. I'm on the verge of losing it.

"Stay on the phone. Listen. We're almost there."

I hear the phone sliding across the floor and more scuffling.
Screaming.
Slamming.
Breaking.

Matt and the other squads fly into the parking lot. We all jump out of the vehicles and start running. What should have been a nineteen minute drive took us less than ten.

"She's screaming! Listen for screaming!" Matt commands.

I stay behind everyone, feeling a little dizzy from both the hit and my rising panic. I scan the area looking for anything that could help. I see a crowd of people gathering near a cabin looking alarmed and murmuring confused at each other.

"There!" I point to the crowd. Matt catches my eye and leads everyone to the crowd. Lyric is right behind him. We all silently follow.

Two of the officers split off and back up the crowd. I stay behind everyone, still on the phone listening to Mariah and Danny.

"Stop fighting me!" Danny screams.

Mariah screams. "Danny, don't shoot! Don't shoot!" She cries and pleads.

I meet Matt's eyes before moving to the front next to. "Gun," I mouth.

Matt nods as he pushes me to the side of the building. "I heard." He pulls an officer next to him. "Gun," he whispers. "We bust through the glass. Lyric leads everyone else in." The other officer nods. Matt quickly gives orders to each person, keeping an eye on me, though we all can hear Mariah and Danny from where we are.

"Danny, you don't want to do this!"

"What did you do? Why did you do this? We could have had something! I killed for you! Don't you understand?"

Matt directs one of our SWAT officers and a couple other officers to the front of the cabin. Lyric positions herself behind Matt.

"Danny, okay. Okay! Just don't shoot! Okay? I'm yours. I'll be yours," Mariah cries.

"Good girl," I whisper. "Make him think he has you."

"It's too late! It's too late! You're just saying that so I won't kill you! But guess what? If I can't have you, no one can!"

"Danny! No!"

Seconds later, Matt crashes through the glass. The entire team follows.

But it's too late.

I hear the gunshot.

Then another. And another.

Several more shots are fired in the chaos, but I don't know if they're from us or him.

I fall to my knees unaware if the screams I hear are Mariah...

...or me...

Chapter Eleven

☆ Mariah ☆

I scream as Danny pulls the trigger. But I have no time to move. I feel the bullet hit me. I fall backwards and to my right side. I know my mouth is open, but I don't know if the scream I'm trying to scream comes out. I clutch my side and chest. There's stabbing pain everywhere. My arm. My shoulder. My chest. My stomach.

I hear more shooting, but with my eyes squeezed shut, I can't tell where it's coming from. I can't even move to get away from it. I feel bullets raining down on me. They're piercing my skin. I try to curl into a ball to protect myself, but I can't. I can feel them all over me.

Usually, I can hear my heart in my ears. But not this time. This time I can't hear it at all.

Did it stop?

Am I dead?

I try to open my eyes, but I can't. All I can hear is silence now. It's cold. Bitterly cold. I can feel myself going into shock. I really don't know at this point if I've even been shot or if my mind just thinks I have been. I feel nothing now. Nothing but the cold.

I shiver and try to focus. But the darkness is so thick. It's hard to breathe in it. It's like I'm being squeezed by a boa constrictor while trying to get air into my lungs with my head shoved into a bucket of paint.

My heart slows further and further until I can't even hold onto the comfort the bitter cold brought me. At least I could feel it. Feel something. Anything.

Please. Not like this. I haven't had any time. It's getting thicker around me. The tiny bit of air I was getting is fading quickly. *I'm sorry, DJ. I'm sorry I wasted so much time. So much time with someone I didn't love when you were here. If only I'd been brave. If only I'd left sooner. If only I'd met you before.* I gasp for air.

"Mariah! Come on. Don't leave me like this!"

DJ.

I can hear his voice in the back of my head, but he sounds so far away.

I try to call up his face in my mind. Anything to hold onto. The image won't come. My arm won't lift. My lungs won't take in any more air.

DJ. I'm sorry. I should've said I love you a long time ago. I knew the first second I saw you. I'm sorry I wasn't brave enough. There's so much I wanted to experience with you. So much I wanted to tell you. Please forgive me. I'm dying. I feel it. I feel you. I feel you surrounding me.

Unable to fight any longer, I allow myself to fade.

DJ is the last thing on my mind, bringing peace as only he knows how.

★★★

My eyes flutter open to blinding lights above me. I whimper and slam my eyes shut, lifting my hand to shield myself.

"Mariah?"

The light blessedly disappears, and I slowly open my eyes again. But I can't speak. I feel like I have a mouth full of gravel and a tongue made of sandpaper. Instead, I whimper again and slowly lower my hand from my eyes.

DJ is sitting next to me looking down at me. His eyes are puffy and red. His cheeks are blotchy. His usually perfect hair is a mess. Like he hasn't washed it in weeks.

His hand is on my cheek, but it's shaky. I reach up and gently take his wrist as I lean into his palm. He runs his thumb over my lower lip before he shifts. He lays his head on my chest and sobs uncontrollably.

"DJ…" I run my fingers through his hair.

"We lost you, Rih. We lost you. And then we got you back. Then we thought we lost you again." He shakes and trembles and hugs me tightly.

"What?" I take a second to look around the room, taking comfort in his embrace. Matt and Lyric are sitting together against the window watching us both. There are machines all over. I look down at the hand I'm running through DJ's hair. I have an IV coming out of it. "What h-happened?"

But DJ doesn't have a chance to answer before doctors rush in. He keeps ahold of my hand, thankfully, as I'm poked and prodded and asked question after question.

When they finally all leave, DJ, Matt and Lyric all sit next to me. DJ runs his thumb gently over the bruise that the IV left in my hand. I'm glad it's out. I'm glad I'm not hooked up to any machines. But I still don't understand what happened.

I take a deep breath. "The last I remember… I was staring down the barrel of Danny's gun."

DJ focuses on my hand. Lyric curls up and lays her head on my thigh. Matt takes my other hand in his.

Matt smiles softly. "You're a fighter. I'll give you that."

"Thank God," DJ whispers.

"I'm in the hospital," I say quietly. "I don't feel like a fighter."

"You are," Matt says. "You really fucking are. When we busted through the glass, he shot. But you threw your arm into his gun. Knocked it away. If you hadn't, he would have hit you in the head."

I look at him, confused. "But I was hit. I remember feeling it."

DJ shakes his head. "No. He didn't hit you. The glass from the patio door rained over you. You got trampled by a couple of guys running in. But he didn't shoot you."

"He tried. But we got him," Matt says.

"You passed out," Lyric says. "We couldn't bring you back. We couldn't even find a pulse at one point."

"We thought you'd been shot," DJ says as he kisses my hand.

"I... thought I had been," I whisper. "I felt it."

Matt shakes his head. "You have some bruises from being hit. And your chest probably hurts from the CPR. But you're okay. We were just waiting for you to wake up." I can tell he's trying to be the strong one for everyone. But I can see how scared he was. How scared he might still be.

"So..., you said you got him...?"

DJ's eyes darken before he leans down. He buries his face in my hair while still holding my hand. Lyric burrows into me. Matt waits until everyone is comfortable before he starts talking, holding my other hand.

"We busted in. We saw him take his shot at you and you throw your arm into his. He shot once before that, though. We think he missed and went back for a second shot. Maybe the first shot scared you. I'm not sure. All I know is we saw you throw your arm against his. The second shot hit the wall. You fell. He pointed the gun back at you. Screamed a bunch of shit. We yelled to drop the gun. He didn't. We shot."

"Demon fucker ended up with sixteen bullet holes," Lyric grumbles.

"Deserved every damn one of them," DJ rumbles against my neck as he kisses it.

"He had files... On all of us. And of people he's killed."

DJ nods into my neck. "All of those people had been reported missing. He was nice enough to leave a detailed written version of what happened to them and where they are. Turns out that the five he killed in your name was the tip of the iceberg. He admitted through the files to three other unsolved missing person cases we've had. One of them being his own mother."

My eyes widen as a realization hits me. "How... long have I been out?"

Matt smiles. "About a day. But you've been in and out. You were still panicking every time you woke up. So they started giving you something for that. Slowly. You were more and more calm."

"I feel like I've been drugged." I let my head fall back as I nuzzle DJ. "My head feels heavy."

"Maybe you need to sleep a little bit," Lyric says as she looks up at me worriedly.

Matt smiles down at her and stands. "Maybe that's our cue to go back to our little hideaway over there." He gestures to the window nook. Lyric reluctantly lets me go and allows Matt to lead her to the nook. But even with my eyes closed, I can feel her watchful eye on me.

DJ lays on the bed and wraps me in his arms. I melt and close my eyes. "He came back so fast." I lean into DJ.

"He had some kind of app on his phone," DJ explains. "It was what the camera feed was going to. We think when he got to Gainesville he checked the feed. Then sped back when he saw you on the phone with us and going through the bags. We can't be sure about that. The only one who really knows that is him. But we did see the app. And the camera feed. It was live. So he could see everything as it was happening."

"He stormed into the room. I heard his tires squeal when he parked next to the cabin. I could hear him running to the room." I feel the hot tears sting my eyes.

"You're safe now. And he's gone. Just rest. Please." DJ hugs me as tightly as he dares as I obey his whispered command and rest.

☆☆☆

(Three Weeks Later)

A few weeks later, after I've fully healed, I carry the last box of my belongings into DJ's house and drop on the floor next to them, groaning and sweating.

"Why is it so hot?" I ask the floor.

DJ laughs as he sits down next to me and slaps my ass. "Because it's Florida. I told you we should have waited to finish until tonight. It's cooler at night."

I giggle at the ass slap and look at him. "You're pretty smart. I should probably listen to you sometimes."

He mock gasps. "You? Actually listen to your boyfriend? Mark the day!"

I laugh as I sit up and look at the mess we've made. "Does this have to be a tonight job? Can this be a tomorrow job? Can tonight be a movie night? With popcorn? And M&Ms?"

He leans in and kisses me. As usual, the kiss lights me on fire. "Tonight can be a whatever you want it to be night."

I smile. "Yes!" I pop up and take off upstairs. I quickly clean up and change into panties and my favorite t-shirt. DJ's Army shirt.

When I come back out of the bathroom and head back downstairs, DJ is sitting on the couch flipping through Netflix shows. He's changed into gray sweats that leave nothing about the size of his dick to the imagination. And he's not wearing a shirt. Which is not fair at all because his chiseled abs are not only droolworthy, but also lickable. Very, very lickable.

I shut my thoughts off and curl into him. He pulls me close to him and kisses the top of my head.

Over the past few weeks, DJ has let me explore him and experiment with him on all things sexual. I feel very inexperienced on so many levels, but DJ doesn't let me feel down about it. He talks me through it. He doesn't make fun of me if I'm doing something wrong. He's honest in what he likes. And he listens to me when I tell him I don't like something. Or if I do.

I'm not used to anything about DJ. I'm not used to being made to feel... special. Wanted. Beautiful. Desired. Sexy. But most of all, I'm not used to feeling loved. I'm not used to feeling such a deep bond with anyone. I'm not used to trusting anyone enough to be myself. To let him have control of any kind.

I've always needed to take care of myself. Even while married, I was the one taking care of anything and everything. Appointments for him. Money. Bills. When I finally decided that I was going to do something for myself, he became such a child about it. An immature, whining child. How dare I do something for me? How dare I do something I enjoy?

I'm not used to being able to relax like this and cuddle. He always said his arm was falling asleep. Or he was too hot. Or sick. Or he didn't want to be touched. But God forbid I didn't want to be touched. Or hugged. Or if I didn't want to cuddle. Then it was always how I never want him to touch me or hug me or cuddle with me.

But not DJ. DJ never turns me away from a hug. He never turns me away when I just want a kiss goodbye. Or when I'm excited to see him when he comes home. He always makes time to cuddle with me. He always tells me I'm pretty. And when I say that I love him, he always says he loves me, too.

DJ never tells me that my writing takes away from time with him. He never tells me that I'm stupid or dumb if I don't remember something. He never gets upset with me if I don't want to go out. But he does push my anxiety a little. He won't let me hibernate. He makes me do some things. Just to get me out of the house.

But he never yells at me if I get panicky. He talks me through it. Makes me feel safe and protected enough to push my limits without the fear of failing. He makes me feel strong enough to get through it. To get through anything.

He's so opposite of all I'm used to that sometimes I can't control how attracted to him he makes me. Suddenly, the movie he's picked seems unimportant and uninteresting. All I can think about is the prize I've come to crave.

I look down and start teasingly tracing the shape of his dick in the thin sweats he's wearing. Why gray sweats look so ridiculously attractive on men is not something I've ever been able to wrap my mind around. But they do. DJ is all the proof I need.

He shifts and reaches down to adjust himself, giving me the access to him I want. I smile and continue tracing patterns on it, then going back to tracing it. I watch, half in wonder and half in lust, as it grows under my touch. Like it always does.

"Looking for something, baby?"

I look up at him. His beautiful green eyes are lit up with all the longing I feel. I smile teasingly. "No… I already found it." I give his dick a gentle squeeze. I love the way it jerks in my palm. I love how his whole body jolts under my touch.

He leans down and kisses me long and passionately as he tugs his sweats down. His tongue slides into my mouth as I start stroking his long length hard and fast. I can feel how close he is already. He always throbs and thickens when he's almost there.

He sucks on my tongue as I pull away. I never thought I'd like the taste of anyone. I didn't like the way my ex tasted. I had no desire to ever try it again.

But not DJ. I love all of him. Including the way he tastes when he comes. Maybe it just takes the right person. I keep stroking him as I shift and take his dick in my mouth with a moan. He tangles my hair around his hand and tugs slightly.

I swirl my tongue around his tip, sucking softly on his dimple just below it. He twitches and pushes me down his length a little. I suck as I bob my head up and down. He comes hard with a low, breathy moan. I smile as I swallow all he gives me.

He tugs my hair gently. I lick him clean before I sit back up looking at him shyly through my lashes. He guides me on top of him so I'm straddling his lap. He slides my panties aside and pushes my hips down on his dick.

I submit fully to him, closing my eyes and wrapping my arms around his shoulders. I'll never get tired of the feeling of him filling me as completely as he does.

He waits until I'm used to his size, which always takes me a few moments. He's so much bigger and thicker than I've ever had, and I love the way it feels when I stretch around him.

I breathe in his scent as I relax. He grips my ass and starts moving me over him. I moan into his neck and dig my nails into his shoulders as he plunges deeply and slowly. He kisses my neck and wraps his arms around my waist. He pulls me to him as I match his pace, meeting each of his delectable thrusts.

"I love the way you feel, beautiful," he says against my neck. "Always so tight and wet for me." His deep, sexy voice against my neck sends shivers throughout my whole body as his lips move against it with each word he says.

"You feel so good, DJ. So good..." I move faster and bounce harder, spreading my legs slightly so I take him deeper into me. Reading me, he picks up the pace.

He hugs me tighter and thrusts harder, deeper, and faster. My body starts to tremble as my thighs quiver. My stomach tightens as my pussy clenches around him. He doesn't stop. Instead, he reaches down and starts rubbing my clit fast and so tantalizingly that when I jerk against him, I nearly come.

But not yet.

I want more. I slide myself back and forth over him as he thrusts just as hard, deep, and fast as he was. Only the infuriatingly sexy man raises the bar when he starts rolling his hips against me.

"Oh God… DJ!" My pussy clamps hard around him. My entire body shudders. I bite his shoulder lightly.

I feel him smile into my neck before he kisses. "Is my girl ready to come?"

I nod. "Please… DJ… Please."

"Come, sexy girl. Come for me." He flicks my clit.

"Ah!" I hit my peak and release explosively around him as I feel him fill my pussy with his come. I convulse against him trying to hang on for dear life. The force of my orgasm has sent me into a whole other dimension where all that exists is me and DJ.

DJ soothingly rubs my back and runs his hands through my hair as I start to come down. I tangle my fingers in his hair as we pant against each other.

After a few moments, I rise off him as I kiss him as deeply as I can, pouring all of the love and affection I have for him into it.

After a long kiss, he settles me back into his side and holds me close. He kisses my forehead. "I love you."

I smile and kiss his chest. "I love you, too."

I don't think I've ever said those words and meant them as deeply as I do when I say them to him. But I do love him. More than anything in the world.

He's my safety.

He's my light.

He's my everything.

Epilogue

☆ DJ ☆

(One Year Later)

"Are you going to tell me where we're going?"

I smile and shake my head as I steer my convertible Mustang through traffic on Highway A1A. "I am not going to tell you. No."

She looks around like she's just landed on a totally new planet. Her eyes are wide. Her mouth is slightly open. Her eyes sparkle with wonder. Her whole body vibrates with excitement at this new adventure.

I glance down at the sun catching the ring on her finger and smile. It's been a year since Mariah became my entire world. A year of everything only getting better than it was the day before. Unbelievable, since every single day with her is the best day of my life.

We got married in a quiet ceremony in my backyard last month. Very quiet. The only people invited to witness our exchange of vows were Matt and Lyric. It was peaceful. Absolutely perfect in every way imaginable.

Mariah has become so close to Lyric that Matt and I often wonder if they share a brain. The bond between them has grown into something to be envious of. They can feel each other's emotions without being in the same room.

A couple of weeks ago, Mariah stopped talking in the middle of a sentence and called Lyric. It turned out Lyric had slipped down the stairs and hit her head. She'd been laying at the bottom of them propped up against the wall. She was dazed. When Matt and I asked Mariah later on how she knew Lyric needed help, she shrugged and simply said I could feel her. If I didn't know any better, I'd think they were twins. It's unbelievable how close they are.

We changed security protocol for any of the signings Mariah attends. We always make sure it's scheduled for a time that me, Lyric, and Matt can be with her. If she takes part in a large signing with other authors, we always take the time off to be with her. None of us, especially me, are willing to allow her to go alone. Not after Danny.

Mariah recovered nicely. She didn't have any scars from the cuts she suffered from the broken glass. I expected she'd never want to leave the house again. But no. Not my girl. She fought through it all and is flourishing as only Mariah can.

She squeaks next to me and grips my thigh as her mouth drops. "DJ, no! Is this that Seven Mile Bridge that goes right over the ocean?"

I smile. "The one and only."

Her nails dig into me as she stares over the vast amount of water on either side of us. "I hate bridges. My heart feels like it's in my mouth."

I gently pry her fingers off my thigh and hold her hand. I kiss her fingers. "I promise you're safe. I know you hate bridges. But you've been doing really well with them. I thought we could push you a little bit. At the end of this is a really nice reward."

She watches the road in front of us quietly as I start the drive across the bridge. "I trust you... I don't trust that." She gestures to the bridge and moves closer to me. She turns her face away from the water on her side of the car and buries her face in my arm.

I kiss the side of her head. "It's really an incredible experience. It's beautiful. I know how much you like beautiful sights."

She nuzzles my arm and takes a deep breath. "Maybe if I focus on that."

"That's my girl. You're safe. I promise. I won't let anything happen to you."

Mariah says nothing. But she does keep hold of my hand. She quietly looks around and takes in the vast gorgeousness that surrounds us. I soothingly run my thumb over the back of her hand and let her adjust.

After a few minutes, she starts to relax. Her grip on my hand loosens. She starts to smile. "It really is pretty."

"It's soothing to me. I like taking long drives, but this one is extra special to me."

She looks up at me. "Why?"

"After my second divorce, I wanted time to myself. I had some time off from work. I was on leave from the Army. It was a coincidence. That doesn't usually happen. If I was on leave, I'd be working. But it worked out that time. I got in the car. And just drove. I hit the A1A down the coast. Then I got on the 1 and kept going. When I hit this bridge, it was like everything just made sense. Everything was calm. Cool. I felt instantly at peace. When I got to the Keys, I ate. Had a drink. Found a hotel. I stayed for a week before I finally decided to head home. But I was in a whole different state of mind. I wasn't angry anymore."

"And now Key West and this bridge hold a special place for you?"

I smile. "I've never shared it with anyone. Never wanted to."

"It really has been a beautiful drive. Even though I feel like I've been in this car for years."

I laugh. "It's a long drive, but it's worth it to see this. I don't care what anyone says. This is one of the Seven Wonders of the World to me."

"Anything that can be built in twenty-two feet of water like this is amazing to me. It doesn't seem like it's that huge of a deal, but it's like four of me deep. And yet here's this structure here that's unmoving and unrelenting. Even though it's been ravished by hurricanes over the past forty years. Yet still. Here it is. Standing tall. Sixty-five feet above the water. Unyielding."

She falls silent as she takes it all in. She relaxes more and more. I smile at knowing my girl well enough to know she'd feel the exact same way about this drive as I do. I'm also proud as yell she knows so much about this bridge, even though it scares the fuck out of her.

When we finally reach our final destination, Mariah is stunned. She looks up at The Reach Resort in utter shock. She does nothing but blink with her mouth partially open. I take her hand and lead her inside so I can check in and get our room key. She stands silently next to me looking around.

I take her hand and our overnight bag that I packed. I lead her to our room. When we get there, I bend and lift her in my arms. She adorably squeaks as she smiles and wraps her arms around my shoulders.

"Have to carry my girl over the threshold." I smile and kiss her as I walk in. I kick the door shut behind me.

"Such a gentleman." She nuzzles my jaw and kisses it.

"Just wait. If you think that was all gentlemanly." I set her down next to the bed and drop our bag.

She looks around the room. "Okay. This… might be the most luxurious room I've ever seen. It has its own sitting room. And a private balcony that overlooks the ocean. I'm sure it costs a fortune."

I smile. "A small fortune." I grab her around the waist, tossing her gently on the bed and crawl on top of her as I kiss her neck and nip it.

She squeals and laughs as she wraps around me. "Why…, Mr. Rens. What can I do for you?"

I nip her neck again and suck as I give her a deep moan. "You, Mrs. Rens. You're all I want."

She arches into me and tilts her head, giving me the access I want. I reach down and pull up her shirt. That one action is all it takes for us both to start tearing off clothes from each other and ourselves.

It doesn't take long before she's naked and writhing underneath me as I hold her wrists above her head and sink deeply into her sexy little pussy with a low possessive growl. I ravish her mouth with mine as our hips slam against each other.

But it's the noises she makes that drive me to the brink. Every damn time. Her breathy whisper of my name. The way she moans. The way she screams out my name when I hit the right spot.

She wraps her legs around me and meets me thrust for thrust. I let go of her wrists and grip her hip. I pull her up into me as I pound into her pussy. She digs her nails in my back and clenches around me, trembling. Her fingernails rake down my back, and she pulls herself and me closer. Like she's trying to crawl inside me because she can't get close enough.

"I fucking love when you do that." I nip her tongue and her suck on her lip, continuing to drive into her over and over.

"DJ! Oh… God… DJ!"

I grip her wrists again, loving how she wiggles against me when I do it. She pushes up on my hand, but she knows she isn't going anywhere. I trail kisses down her collarbone to her tits and nip each of them before taking one nipple into my mouth and sucking. Hard. It causes her to buck up into me. Just the way I like it.

"Mmm...," I moan against her skin. I kiss her nipples and thrust harder, deeper, and faster. I roll my hips against her because I've learned very well that it pushes her straight to the edge. Right where I need her to be.

She screams and throws her body into mine. I cover her mouth with mine to muffle the screams before they get too loud.

"DJ..." Her tongue meets mine in a frenzied dance. "DJ... I'm... gonna...."

I smile into the kiss. "Come. Come for me, my beautiful wife."

The command is all it takes. She throws her head back as I slam into her pussy. I kiss her hard as she comes for me. Her pulsing and clenching as she tightens around me drags my orgasm from me. I couldn't stop it if I tried. Not that I'd ever want to.

Our hips grind against each other as our powerful releases rip through us. I slow my thrusts helping us both to come down. I wrap my arms around her, letting go of her wrists as I lay on top of her holding her close while we both pant against each other's neck in an attempt to catch our breath.

After several moments, I roll off her and pull her next to me. I hold her as closely and tightly as possible. She curls happily in my arms and lets out a very sexy, content sigh.

I'm impressed and proud of her each and every day. She's so strong to be able to fight the anxiety and panic that lives within her. To be able to come through all of the emotional and mental abuse she's dealt with over the years by the people who promised to love her and vowed to protect her is something I admire about her.

But the thing I'm most happy about is that we both found what we've been looking for. For so many years we settled for a life neither of us wanted. And while I had been content, I realized that my life was meaningless without her. That I had only been going through the motions. Not really noticing what was happening around me.

She brings the light to my world that I was missing. The warmth to the frosty bitterness that surrounded me. Mariah is quite literally the other half of me. The part I knew I was missing, but had never been able to find the right person to fill in the void.

Mariah is my life.

My love.

The one person I'd never be able to survive without.

My heart.

My Heaven.

The End

Next In The Beautiful Dream Series

The sweet and sinfully sexy Beautiful Dream Series continues with
Breaking Boundaries.

Matt:

My tenacity and decision-making skills are two of the things that make me
a good Lieutenant. Until Lyric Sharpe shows up to ruin my day. And just
because I'm a glutton for punishment, I had to go and add a drunken night
with my best friend, Captain DJ Rens, into the mix to top off the sudden
feelings I've grown for my friend with benefits, Mariah Carter. This isn't
going to end well.

Lyric:

Men can't handle me. I'm far too sassy, and too much of a brat. When
Matt, my direct commanding officer, shows interest in me, I'm thrown for
a loop. But I have a serious thing for my roommate, Mariah, and my
Captain, DJ.

DJ:

When I became a Captain, I did it with the stipulation that I still be allowed
to do patrol. When Mariah enters my life, I regret everything about that
decision. Now, she's all I want. Well, her, Matt, and Lyric.

Mariah:

After a drunken night of mind-blowing passion with Lyric I hoped would
end the feelings I have for DJ and Matt, I realized those feelings aren't
going away. Everything comes to light with our lives on the line…

Order ***Breaking Boundaries*** Today!

The Beautiful Dream Series

Available Now

Loving You
My Love, My Heart
Softening Lyric
Undercover Temptations
Captain Charming
Breaking Boundaries
Crashing Into You
Tactical Inferno
Ravishing Our Queen
Cherished By The Texan
Unveiling Our Passions

Box Sets Available

The Beautiful Dream Series: Box Set: Part 1
The Beautiful Dream Series: Box Set: Part 2

Other Books By Melony Ann
The Crane Family Series

Available Now

The Reluctant Mafia King
Sweet Lies
Billion Dollar Love Story
Be Mine
Protecting Her
Dangerously Forbidden Love
His Heart
Love In The Dark

Box Sets Available

The Crane Family Series

The Deimos Trilogy

Available Now

Connor's Legacy
Aryan's Alpha
Kade's Redemption

Box Sets Available

The Deimos Trilogy

The Forbidden Temptation Series

Available Now

The Detective's Forbidden Temptation
The Running Back's Forbidden Temptation

The Lucinio Family Series

Available Now

Rising From The Ashes
The Player's Rebel
Encrypting My Heart
Fighting My Fate

Multi Author Series
Piper Falls: Firehouse 49

Available Now

Ignite My Fire by Melony Ann
Regain My Fire by Kindra White
Playing With My Fire by D.L. Howe
Fight My Fire by Darley Collins
Against My Fire by Anneke Boshoff
Relight My Fire by Louise Murchie
Harness My Fire by Ayana Lisbet
Quench My Fire by Havana Wilder

Let's Be Friends

Follow me on

Bookbub

Facebook

Goodreads

Instagram

Tik Tok

Visit my website
www.melonyannauthor.com

Subscribe to my newsletter and get a FREE never-seen-before NOVELLA
just for subscribers!
https://www.melonyannauthor.com/exclusive-content

Join my Facebook Reader Group!
Melony Ann's Sizzling Book Nook
https://www.facebook.com/groups/melonyannssizzlingbooknook

The official Beautiful Dream Series Playlist on YouTube
https://youtube.com/playlist?list=PLGEiD5wbQmDe1z4_FeeKbMLcBkOz
1M4L4

Dedication

When the darkness overtakes us, we know you'll always come for us.

Acknowledgements

Brad - Words always seem to fail me when I'm trying to thank you for everything you do for me. I wouldn't be where I am without you and your love and support. You believe so much in me and my work that you've thrown so much into this. I love you. More than I can ever explain to you.

Laura - I'm beyond impressed with your talent with all of the covers and posts that you create for me. I'm so proud of you and the success you've seen in only a few months. You deserve all of it. I love you so very much that sometimes I wonder if it's legal.

Jay - When I think of what's happened, I have to stop and catch my breath. It's like a whirlwind of amazingness. You're so patient with us. Your love is all encompassing. You stepped up and made everything easy, even though what we all have should be complicated as fuck. I love everything about you. I love you.

Anneke - Can you just be in the US already? I need my Anneke.

Jason - Near or far, thank you for being here.

Kayla - I think you need to be closer. Move here. We can make snow angels and make fun of everyone in all of their heavy snow gear that makes them look like the bundled up kid from *A Christmas Story*.

To the Bookstagram Community.

To my family.

To all of those who believe in me and support me.

To all of those who don't.

Cover by: Carter Cover Designs

Edited by: Alyssa Skaggs

About Melony Ann

Melony Ann began writing short stories and poetry as a child. She continued honing her craft over the years until she took the plunge and began publishing her work, despite having severe anxiety.

Melony writes contemporary romance stories that are full of suspense and a lot of steam.

When she isn't writing, she is loving her family and working to make her life something she deserves.

Melony believes that if her writing can inspire just one person, then all of her hard work is worth it.

Her hope is that her writing allows each and every one of her readers to escape for a little while. To dive into a different world one book at a time.

www.ingramcontent.com/pod-product-compliance
Lightning Source LLC
Chambersburg PA
CBHW050737230626

47052CB00003BA/513